In Times of Siege

The Thousand Faces of Night
The Art of Dying
The Ghosts of Vasu Master
When Dreams Travel
A Southern Harvest (ed.)
Sorry, Best Friend! (coedited with Shama Futehally)

In Times of Siege

GITHA HARIHARAN

Pantheon Books, New York

Library of Congress Cataloging-in-Publication Data
Githa Hariharan.
In times of siege / Githa Hariharan.
p. cm.
ISBN 0-375-42239-0
1. College teachers—Fiction. 2. Religious fundamentalism—Fiction.
3. New Delhi (India)—Fiction. 4. Guardian and ward—Fiction.
5. Middle-aged men—Fiction. 6. Young women—Fiction. I. Title.
PR9499.3.G5815 2003
823'.914—dc21   2003042017

www.pantheonbooks.com

Book design by Soonyoung Kwon

Printed in the United States of America

First American Edition

2   4   5   6   9   7   5   3   1

For all those who speak up in times of siege

Look at them,
busy, making an iron frame
for a bubble on the water
to make it safe!

—Basava, vachana 162

and if the City falls but a single man escapes
he will carry the City within himself on the roads of exile
he will be the City

—Zbigniew Herbert, "Report from the Besieged City"

If you risk your hand
with a cobra in a pitcher
will it let you
pass?

—Basava, vachana 212

In Times of Siege

ONE

New Delhi

AUGUST 23, 2000

*S*outh Gate. Shiv's car slows down, goes past the security booth, then over a series of unmarked humps. A ramshackle old Fiat passes by.

Ahead a wheezing bus snorts its way toward him. A cycle follows.

Otherwise the road, as far as he can see, is setting for more human traffic. Boys and girls—or, he corrects himself, young men and women. Dozens of them, some sitting on the pavement, staring frankly at the world going by, some daydreaming at the bus stop. A few clustered round the dhaba by the road, drinking tea and smoking. Though he is the visitor, it is they who look at him like well-briefed sightseers viewing a tourist staple. A teacher, a faculty type, a familiar monument in a city of ruins.

The university. A gate, a winding road, young faces, straight limbs. The city yields its claims. Delhi, an insatiable amoeba that grows in all directions, recedes.

Here too the trees and bushes that border the road on either side look vulnerable to the spite of the late summer sun. But the university's green—prolific, variegated—has penetrated the landscape into the heart of its texture. Here green fingers colonize the buildings. Brick is generously streaked with ivy and creepers, or curtained by clumps of untrimmed bushes. Though Shiv can't tell from the road, the buildings look as if they might be hospitable to birds' nests, cobwebs, beehives.

He feels a twinge of wonder and excitement, like a boy hungry for adventure, a castaway in an island where all the natives are young. An island in landlocked Delhi, no mean marvel. You could arrive here from the railway station, a pliant piece of clay to be molded, live the last and best years of childhood. Then take a direct bus, the 615, to deliver you back at the station. Delhi need be seen only from a bus window, its imperial avenues, its filth-ridden hovels and concrete monstrosities reduced to the powerless, fleeting images of a dream.

He sees two girls—no, a woman and a girl—wave at him to stop.

Though the hostel he is going to cannot be far away, he slows down and comes to a halt. The younger one runs up to his window, her long hair and her diaphanous blue dupatta flying behind her.

"Are you going up-campus?" she asks. Her voice is shrill and breathless.

He is tempted to find out how far he will have to go, which hill he will have to climb to reach this up-campus. But he shakes his head, apologizes.

She turns to pull a face at the other woman who is already peering into the distance, on the lookout for another car.

"I am looking for a hostel," he tells the girl and she turns back to him impatiently. "Jamuna Ladies' Hostel—I mean women's hostel. Would you tell me where that is?"

She points to a building behind the trees, then runs back to her companion.

The hostel building is at the end of a lane to the left. Its face is lined with balconies full of clothes hung out to dry. He parks under a tree, fitting the car neatly into a small patch of shade, and walks slowly to the open gate. He waits till he sees a girl going in. Her back is a jar-shape stuffed into faded blue jeans.

"Please," he says to the jar, and it turns around, revealing a moonface that belongs in an old Hindi film. "Please," he says to this siren in the wrong costume, "could you tell Meena, R. Meena, that her guardian is waiting for her at the gate?"

Moonface looks him up and down with undisguised curiosity. "She's broken her knee," she volunteers.

"I know, that's why I am here. I've come to take her home."

The girl nods at him. From her face it is clear that her curiosity has been instantly appeased. She disappears into the building.

Shiv stands there, looking around him.

Though he too lives in a university, it is a world apart from this living, breathing mass of students. Where he teaches, only the teachers are visible. The students are names, addresses, postmarks. Part of what is called, oddly, an Open University, as if the gates are perpetually open and the students have wandered away. Though there are no resident students, his campus is even

(5)

larger than this one. He lives at the south end of his campus, a rocky, partially cleared stretch of jungle that the professors share with noisy peacocks, and the occasional snake, jackal and monkey. He drives to the "academic complex" in the north part of the campus, to sit every day in an office with an intimidating bilingual nameplate on the door: Professor Shivamurthy in English, Shiv Murthy in Hindi. He is, at fifty-two, finally a professor of history, though not quite the sort his father imagined in daydreams on his behalf. He no longer teaches students; as his Department Head likes to put it, he coordinates resources for his educational clients.

Shiv shifts from leg to leg restlessly. He can sense someone watching him.

He turns around and notices a tiny makeshift shop across the road, nestled under a tree. It sells newspapers, cigarettes, and the garishly colored packets of junk food that have been hung out on display.

The shopkeeper, a young man in need of excitement, stands outside his shop staring at Shiv. His gaze is hopeful, as if he expects Shiv to do something in the next few minutes that will make today less boring than yesterday. Then, as the young man watches Shiv do nothing, he moves his hand casually toward his crotch and scratches himself. The expectant look on his face turns thoughtful.

Shiv concedes defeat in their staring competition and turns back to the hostel gate. There is no guard at the gate, though he is sure there is usually one, the sort with a lathi, protecting that holy of holies, a girls' hostel. Perhaps he should waylay someone else going into the hostel and ask her why the girl is taking so long.

. . .

The girl. When she first came to Kamala Nehru University in Delhi two, three years back, her mother wrote to Shiv asking if he would be her daughter's "local guardian." He didn't know what this would involve, and quickly passed the letter to Rekha. His wife, Rekha, with the efficiency that makes her an administrative asset in her office, took over. Not that she had much to do. She picked up the girl from her hostel on a Sunday and took her to Sarojini Nagar to buy bargain woolens for her first Delhi winter. Then brought her home for lunch.

The girl did not have much to say for herself—Shiv can't remember having a conversation with her. She seemed watchful though, as if assessing their faces, their words, the spare but impeccable living room, their hospitality. About the only thing Shiv recalls is her silent but enthusiastic feeding at lunch. Rekha called her a few times after that, and perhaps the girl did come home again, though he is not sure of that. He does remember that the girl seemed self-sufficient. She was always too busy to visit them on Sundays—the only day Rekha could have guests for lunch—and Shiv had all but forgotten he was her guardian till the telephone call yesterday.

"You don't know me," said a girl's voice on the phone. "I am a friend of Meena's."

It took Shiv a moment to remember who Meena was. Then foolishly he said the first thing that came to his mind. "I am sorry," he said. "My wife is not in town."

There was a nonplussed silence from the girl, and he recovered himself to ask, "Is something wrong? Is Meena all right?"

The girl replied in a burst of relief, "No, she's not. She fell off a bus and she's broken her knee. She wants you to come and get her from the hostel. Jamuna Ladies' Hostel. Room 15. It's very difficult for her here, she has a huge cast and she can't manage. When can you come?"

"Tomorrow. Tomorrow afternoon. How long will she be in the cast?"

"I'm not sure, but I think the doctor said at least three or four weeks. I'll pack her things for her by tomorrow."

Shiv moves closer to the open gate, peers in. Why is the girl taking so long? He was hoping to take her home, settle her in the room downstairs, and get back to the Department. (They may not have classroom hours where he teaches, but they are devoted to office hours.) If the girl needs anything while he is away, there's Kamla in the servants' quarters at the back. And tonight he will have to call her parents if she hasn't already done that. Her parents will probably want to take her home, though he will, for the sake of courtesy, offer to have mother and daughter stay with him till Meena is better. But really, without Rekha, two guests in the house, one with a broken leg—Shiv steps into the hostel grounds warily, half expecting someone to emerge from the building and stop him from taking a step further.

Then three girls emerge as if on signal; one of them is Meena on crutches. Shiv forgets his fear of rules in girls' hostels and goes toward them.

As he approaches them, all three girls stop and look at him. The frame freezes there.

Shiv will always remember this image, three girls, a stranger on either side of Meena, a look in their unblinking eyes that makes him hesitate—as if he is on the brink of something,

something that cannot be undone. He will always remember the silent challenge in their eyes: Here you are, the man, the savior of one-legged girls. Well? Do what you have to, act your role!

Then Shiv sees the small battered suitcase, and he is able to move again, having seen where his task lies. He takes the suitcase from the girl holding it; it is surprisingly light. His ward travels light, unlike his wife and daughter, both of whom pack heavily and comprehensively for all occasions.

They move in a slow, solemn procession to the car; Shiv leads the way with the suitcase. He opens the nearest door to the backseat and waits.

"How do I get in?" These are Meena's first words to him. Only now it occurs to him that they have not greeted each other, nor has she thanked him for coming. Shiv's heart sinks; it is bad enough to have to play good Samaritan, but to cope with silence and perhaps sullenness as well?

"Sit on the edge of the seat, sideways, then crawl back on your bum," advises one of the girls. Clearly she is the competent sort who always knows what she is talking about.

Meena does this, slowly, the muscles on her face taut with the strain, her mouth open, breathing shallowly. Shiv shuts the door gently but still he sees her wince. His Maruti is too small for a body; he sees this for the first time. She sits as if boxed in a cupboard shelf, her feet flexed against the car door.

"All right?" he asks, and unexpectedly, she smiles a sweet, rueful smile.

"No, but let's go," she replies.

Shiv drives self-consciously, aware of her discomfort every time he goes over a hump or into a pothole. "Sorry," he says a few times, but then it seems pointless. The road is an obstacle course all the way from her KNU, a vibrant island of green, to the arid stretches of his KGU.

Shiv can sense the overwhelming relief in the car, his and hers, as they finally approach his driveway an hour later.

Getting out of the car proves more difficult than getting in, especially without the practical friend's advice. Shiv holds the girl's moist, clammy hand while she grunts her way forward to the edge of the seat. Then with a final grunt she pulls herself up and totters on one foot. He holds on to her, looking round wildly for the crutches. She is heavier than he expected. With her weight on him, Shiv too can feel a groan coming to his lips—as if it is infectious—and he leans forward to get the crutches lying on the car floor.

The wooden crutches are relics from a medieval medical kit. They belong ostentatiously to a past that has long been used up. The stuffing on top of one has entirely given way. Its entrails hang out, desolate twisted rags. The cushion of the other crutch has patches of its original covering, midway in the process of green turning to brown. The fake leather covering has an oily look to it, memories of the many armpits it has supported. The two crutches are of unequal height, and one has lost its rubber foot.

Shiv and the girl move together clumsily to the front door and he hastens to unlock it.

Now that she is here, Shiv's preparations seem woefully inadequate. He has made the bed in the little room downstairs, remembered to keep a bottle of water and a glass on the table by the bed. But the room that greets them is a small dark hole. He can see the dust on the table around the bottle. A pair of large, elegant mosquitoes sit on the wall by the bed like a reception committee.

But she does not seem to notice any of this. He can hear her sigh as he helps her into bed. She stretches out her legs and shuts her eyes.

Shiv hesitates, wondering if he should cover her, or get her something to eat or drink. He waits, but her eyes remain shut. Shiv notices two little holes side by side on her faded gray T-shirt. Her face, a smooth brown mask, looks young and weary, a combination he has not seen before.

On an impulse, Shiv leaves the room and goes looking for Rekha's brass bell, a bell his mother used at her endless pujas to call the deaf gods to attention. The bell, having failed to perform its real function, now sits polished and gleaming, an object on exhibit in the living room of a nonpraying household. Its magic may have failed, but it does well as an arty object. Shiv returns with the bell, places it by the water bottle on the table. He puts away the ancient crutches in a corner and keeps a walking stick instead by her bed.

He takes one more look at her, willing her to open her eyes and say something. But she remains still, oblivious of his presence. Suddenly Shiv feels like an intruder in his own house. He switches off the lamp on the table and leaves the room, half-shutting the door behind him.

TWO

AUGUST 24

When Shiv opens his eyes, he immediately feels something out of place in the silence. He has not set the alarm, but he has woken up as always, at the stroke of six.

The house sits silent, but he can hear—or sense—its brooding on the day to come.

The girl must be asleep. Should he ask her if she drinks tea, coffee? Or does she still drink milk? His daughter hated milk when she was a child and they had to disguise it with all kinds of synthetic chocolatey powders. Energy drinks, they are called. Should he go ask the girl if she would like an energy drink?

He still thinks of her as *the girl,* she has not yet become a person with a name.

Shiv stirs the sugar in his tea and takes the cup to his mouth when he hears the bell. Then he hears her call. She calls him professor; it is as if she has heard him thinking of her as the girl.

The girl's voice, high-pitched and desperate, repeats, "Professor!"

He puts down the cup clumsily, splashes tea on Rekha's off-white tablecloth, and hurries downstairs.

The girl doesn't look grateful to see him. If anything, she has an impatient look on her face as if to say, Where were you? Didn't you hear me call?

"Did you want something?" Shiv asks her.

She has pulled the sheets aside and is sitting up, frowning at her leg. "Of course," she snaps, then adds plaintively, "I have to go to the bathroom."

He helps her up, gives her the walking stick by the chair, his father's old walking stick. She gasps with pain; it's impossible to use the stick without putting some weight on her broken leg. Shiv takes the stick from her and hands her the decrepit crutches. He walks at her snail's pace, taking her weight on his arm and shoulder.

Once they are in the bathroom, he is not sure what to do. But she has apparently thought it out. She leans the crutches against the wall, tests her balance on the good leg. "Shut the door," she says. "Please wait outside for me."

As he shuts the door, he hears her groan with the effort of easing herself down to a sitting position. Then he hears a steady, trickling sound. He feels like an eavesdropper, but he continues to stand by the door. "I'll buy a pair of crutches today," he says.

She doesn't reply. Or if she does, the sudden sound of tap water filling the bucket drowns out her words.

Shiv goes up the winding stairs to the landing outside the servants' quarters. "Quarters" is a grand way to describe the room Kamla, her husband and their daughter live in. The husband is out all day working as an office peon. Shiv and Rekha rarely see him. The family lives here on condition that Kamla comes in twice a day, once to clean, once to cook. She is finicky about following this spoken contract to the letter, lest Shiv and Rekha think the quarters entitle them to her services any time of the day or night.

The radio in Kamla's room blares a film song but the door remains shut despite Shiv's knocking. He calls aloud, for good measure, both mother and daughter: "Kamla! Babli!"

No response.

He thinks he hears Meena call.

Flustered, he pushes the door open. Inside, lit by the beam of sunlight the open door has let in, he sees an idyllic domestic scene. Kamla is in the corner of the room that serves as a kitchen, sitting on her haunches before the stove. Babli, dressed and ready in her blue and white school uniform, extravagant white ribbons in her hair, is on the floor, studying. The whirring of the table fan, the smoky kitchen corner and the music are a heady combination. Shiv has to make an effort to recall his sense of irritation and urgency.

"Kamla, you will have to come down and help the girl," he says. "In the bathroom," he adds, to make it clear that this is women's business.

Kamla looks pained. Kamla has a special look, a look of virtuous suffering that invariably makes Shiv feel guilty about asking her to do something. Not that he ever has to. Usually meals and teas appear on the dining table as if by magic even when Rekha is at the office. Shiv has never seen Kamla clean his study, so he assumes it is done when he is not there. Rekha has shopped for the ten or twelve weeks she will be away. She has left detailed instructions with Kamla; the freezer is full despite the unreliable power situation. But even Rekha, with all her efficiency and foresight, could not have anticipated Meena's unexpected arrival.

Now Kamla hastily puts away rotis in a box and gets up. "Babli, shut the door when you go," she says. "And don't forget your tiffin box."

Babli ignores her and asks Shiv, "What happened to the didi downstairs?"

Later he asks Meena Babli's question.

Meena has changed her clothes. She now wears a bright red T-shirt and a long crinkled and flowery skirt. She looks well-scrubbed though she has only had a pretend-bath. Before Kamla left with the wet towel and empty basin, she must have combed Meena's hair and plaited it tightly. The result is a slightly older (and larger) version of Babli sitting up in bed, considering Shiv's question.

"So what happened? How did you manage to fall off the bus?"

"I don't know how I slipped. I still can't believe it—it wasn't as if anyone was pushing me. That's happened hundreds of times and I've never fallen."

"But was the bus moving?" This frightening possibility has just occurred to Shiv. It's been at least twenty years since he was squeezed into a Delhi bus.

"No, of course not. Otherwise you would have been arranging my funeral now." She smiles shrewdly at the alarm on his face. "What a waste," she then sighs. "If only it had been at a rally or something. You know, if it had been the fault of the police, breaking a leg would have been of some use."

Shiv is taken aback by this sample of her wishful thinking

but also engaged by it. So the cause—whatever hers is—is worth a broken leg? Why has he never seen this Meena before?

"Look, I know you plan to call my parents." She slips this in casually, though she is watching him carefully. "I'd rather you didn't. That you didn't worry them. I'll be all right here. You don't mind, do you?"

Shiv is completely unprepared for this. But she is waiting for him to decide, holding back eagerness and anxiety. The worldly-wise smile and all other hints of shrewdness have left her face.

"Of course, if you want to stay here . . ." Shiv finds himself saying to her. "I think we should speak to your parents, you would be more comfortable with your mother here. Kamla can be quite elusive if Rekha is not here. But let's see. Let's see how it goes for a few days."

"I don't need Kamla, she's too slow and clumsy. But you're here, aren't you? Since you don't have to meet your students, can't you bring your work home? I mean—if you don't mind?"

At the Department, Shiv unlocks his room and finds several notes that have been pushed under the door. He picks up the dusty bits of paper and sees that one is a reminder to attend a meeting at noon. Another is a long list of Items for Discussion. If he had remembered the meeting, maybe he wouldn't have left Meena to Kamla's mercy. When Rekha is not in town, Kamla develops a host of handicaps, beginning with deafness.

As usual Shiv is the last one at the meeting. The Department Head, his four colleagues, and a secretary armed with pad and pen are already there. The Head sits with his secretary next to him like a handmaiden; facing them are his colleagues, Lal,

Arya, Menon, and Amita Sen. The core faculty, processors of historical resources for their unseen students.

The ubiquitous beverage, a creative fusion of tea and coffee, has already arrived in chipped white cups and saucers. Everyone waits as always for the secretary to play mother and pass the cups around. Though Shiv gives her a sympathetic smile she hands him a particularly loathsome cup. Not only is it chipped, it is also stained on the edge. Some of the lukewarm brown liquid has splashed on to the saucer. What is left in the cup has a circle of wrinkled skin floating on its surface. The secretary too looks at Shiv's cup, then looks apologetic. He takes the cup and saucer from her and puts them back on the table. Then he sits down next to Amita (who gives him a quick conspiratorial grin) and he unfolds the slip of paper with the items for discussion. Out of twelve, seven are marked with asterisks to illustrate their importance.

"Shall we begin?" asks the Head, clearing his throat.

The tubelight flickers.

The Head frowns at the light and it obediently settles down. A small triumph in a small life. The Head, Dr. Sharma, is a timid man whose head is just a little too big for his slight, finely sculpted body. His idea of paradise would be a place where the inmates proceed solemnly from one meeting to another. He is now practicing for his role in his own corner of paradise: presiding, unbearably grave and pompous.

"Our biggest problem at this juncture is maintenance of the computers and printers. You are all aware that this is expensive, state-of-the-art equipment." (Shiv wonders if this is what Administration told him and if he really believes it.) "But in the past week one printer was left working all night with a month's supply of paper completely twisted out of shape. There is also the problem of outsiders using the computer facilities. What I put to you today is one possible solution: should we appoint a Vigilance Officer from among us to check all the equipment first thing in the morning and last thing at night?"

Everyone looks at his or her papers with firm concentration, waiting for the inevitable volunteer. Dr. Kishan Lal obliges. "I will need a set of keys," he tells the Head, who in turn asks the furiously writing secretary to make a note of it.

"Then there is the business of the coolers," says the Head. "Administration has sent a memo which the Dean has forwarded to me—let me see, here it is—All Department Heads may kindly fill in particulars re. the condition of the Department coolers. This is to ensure that repairs are carried out in good time for the summer season."

The Head pauses; he is the only one of them with air-conditioning in his room, and the poor man is always nervous about a mutiny among his coolerwalla colleagues.

Dr. Lal now feels compelled to observe with a profound air, "It is almost September . . ."

"A little late for this year, but maybe for next summer?" says the Head, slipping the memo under his pile of papers.

On cue, the power goes. Everyone stirs restlessly while the secretary opens curtains, windows, door.

Shaded by semidarkness, his sheaf of papers doubling as a hand-fan, Shiv yawns luxuriously as they proceed through the other items.

Lesson and module deadlines. The fax machine is misbehaving again. Three hundred and seventy-six assignments have been lost in the post. Stationery sanctions once again: they were short of pens in last week's National Movements course writers' meeting.

By the time the power comes back and the fans and cooler stir into frenetic, whirling life, they are down to the last item. An innocent catchall heading minus asterisk, Any Other Matters for Discussion.

The Head looks down modestly at his papers and says, "I am aware of the fact that this is a general administrative meeting, not a course team meeting. But with your permission, Dr. Menon, as In-Charge of the Modern India course, and yours, Dr. Murthy, as In-Charge of the B.A. History program—we have a rather delicate item to take up now. Dr. Arya has brought it to my notice that some faculty members may be overstepping their bounds. Or should I say, overusing their editorial pencils."

Shiv can see Arya steal a look at Menon.

It's only recently that Arya has been promoted to being addressed as Doctor. Though Shiv still doesn't know where the man got a doctorate from, or even if he has one in the first place. Arya was a mousy dogsbody for years—Kishan Lal's predecessor in the volunteering hotseat. But over the last year or two, he has been revealing a more aggressive face, unveiling one tantalizing feature at a time. Shiv has heard rumors of the weekly meetings in Arya's house on campus; he has heard that the guests have been seen leaving the house in khaki gear. Certainly Arya has acquired a new look. His face, once hangdog and apologetic, now seems devoid of flab. Leaner, meaner.

But whatever his new look and connections, it is difficult to take Arya seriously. To see Arya as academic. Or Arya as the enemy-in-training. To believe in Arya the historian. (Though many of them only edit what other historians write, the word *historian*—something of a touchstone, an ideal—is never absent from their minds.)

Arya is now trying out his new persona in public. He has actually taken the trouble to read a lesson, part of one of the modules on Modern India; and he claims that it has been unfairly edited. "Cut and slashed," he says, glowering in the general direction of Menon, Amita and Shiv. His open mouth reveals illicitly large teeth, long like those of a hungry wolf. "Why ask an eminent historian to write a lesson if we are going to do whatever we like with it?"

Like Arya, the eminent historian is a pamphleteer who has recently turned into a scholar.

The Head, his eyes carefully neutral, turns to Menon. Menon is a thin, taciturn man with a heap of curls on his head and a lush beard. All this hair and the clothes he wears—always a couple of sizes too big for him—are part of his camouflage system. "Dr. Menon?" the Head now says, trying not to be irritated by the fact that Menon is looking up into space and not at him. "Maybe you could tell us what the problem was?"

Menon tears himself away from the ceiling. He makes a quick calculation or two though his face remains unreadable. "I thought it best to steer clear of controversial statements," he says. (Menon knows this will appeal to the Head.) "The author had made one or two questionable statements on minority communities and I excised those. I don't recall actually rewriting anything."

But Arya pipes in angrily, "Maybe Dr. Menon needs to refresh his memory. I have the material right here. A whole paragraph, a key paragraph, has been dropped from an important section: 'Problems of the Country and Their Solutions.'"

He proceeds to read every jewel-encrusted word of the paragraph. "Our land has always been a temptation to greedy marauders, barbarous invaders and oppressive rulers. This story of invasion and resistance is three thousand years old. Hundreds of thousands of foreigners found their way to India during these thousands of years, but they all suffered humiliating defeat. Some of them we digested. When we were disunited, we failed to recognize who were our own and who were foreigners, and we were unable to digest them. Today, apart from Muslims, even Christians, Parsis and other foreigners are also recognized as minority communities. But in many of the states the Hindus have been reduced to a minority, and the Muslims, Christians or Sikhs are in a majority."

There is an uncomfortable silence.

The secretary, Mrs. Khan, is a Muslim. Arya must remember this too, though each time he says the words "foreigner" or "Muslim" he spits them out like something sour in his mouth. Shiv can see that all of them are looking at Mrs. Khan with some sort of fascinated horror. The secretary's face is impassive, bent over her pad. She seems to be writing down every word as if her life depends on it.

The Head's face is pinched with anxiety; meetings in paradise do not slip out of control. "Mrs. Khan," he says to the bent head, "I don't think we need keep you any longer. I know you have work piled up on your table—oh, I have also asked Administration to send the temp we asked for. She will come in today so you can familiarize her with the office work."

The secretary is out of the room in a flash; she does not stop to pick up the empty cups and saucers from the table.

The Head sighs; even he sees that this meeting must be

brought to an end. "I think we will sort out this little matter more easily if—if Dr. Menon and Dr. Arya have a healthy dialogue. In my room, say in about half an hour?"

Back in his room, Shiv discovers a nice coincidence: a notice in his In-tray tells him Mrs. Khan is going on casual leave from the next day. Obviously the leave was planned many days back. But now she has about a week to recover from the new status thrust on her—Muslim Mrs. Khan, Foreign Mrs. Khan. Mrs. Khan, a woman who has travelled leagues from her grandmother's and mother's lives to work in an office and make a modest contribution to the family income. Now she is being pushed back to square one, to the old diminishing religious identity. She has a few days to examine her new status and, hopefully, shed it. To come back the same sweet, helpful secretary they know, incorrigible only when it comes to telling *n*'s and *u*'s apart on her typewriter.

Shiv frowns at his In-tray. Suddenly he wants to get away from the Department. He does have to leave early anyway to buy Meena's crutches. He should go home and see how she is managing. And he has to decide what to do about ringing up her mother. Decide about Meena staying on.

Amita Sen walks in, catches his frown. "Faculty meeting blues?" she asks in mock sympathy, though Shiv knows she is here to exorcise her own disgust at the combination of coolers and Arya's idiocies taking up a whole morning of her life.

When he doesn't respond, she shrugs, lights a cigarette, and studies his face.

"You look like you could use a field trip to the real world," she says. "What do you say we run away for lunch—I know a good little place at least fifteen kilometers from the Department. Is that far enough for you?"

Amita and Shiv have slept with each other a few times. But perhaps "slept with each other" is inaccurate. They have, on four occasions, had extended lunches; lunches which have extended to hurried, unsatisfying sex at her house. All four times she lay in bed afterwards, her face veiled by cigarette smoke, watching him dress; each time he let himself out of the house and got back to the Department, feeling like a truant schoolboy.

Amita's greatest fear is boredom. And loneliness, she has found, is usually accompanied by boredom. Her husband is a successful chartered accountant; he holds the income tax secrets of many rich and powerful men in his files. Amita and Shiv have never spoken of him, but Shiv doubts that the man has ever tried to unravel his wife's melancholy file of accounts.

Now Shiv says to her, gently, "I can't. My ward—an old family friend's daughter—is at my place with a broken leg. In fact, I am going to have to apply for leave. Her parents have asked me to look after her. And I have done nothing for her all the years she has been in Delhi."

Amita's thin eyebrows go up and she stubs out her cigarette. Shiv can tell she is hurt, but she is gamely sticking to the unspoken rules of their relationship—or whatever halfhearted little thing there is between them.

As Shiv drives to Yusuf Sarai to look for a pair of crutches, he is filled with an absurd sense of well-being. The briefcase on the backseat is stuffed with papers. His copy of the leave application—privilege leave for personal reasons—is in the briefcase, along with notes for a new lesson to be written, other lessons to be edited, and assignments to be corrected and graded. He has stopped worrying about informing Meena's parents. After all, the girl is in her twenties, she must be allowed to make her own decisions. And Meena, from what Shiv has seen of her for a day, certainly seems to know her own mind.

As he slows down for the traffic lights ahead, he becomes aware of a persistent honking behind him.

Shiv looks into the rearview mirror and glimpses a large white car bearing down on him, and then it disappears from view. A second later it is alongside him to the left; a noisy, brash whale edging him out, a plebeian Maruti fish. He hangs on, trying not to be pushed in the way of cars zooming down the road on the other side.

The white car is now abreast of his so that Shiv can see the grinning occupants. Three boys, the one at the wheel with blow-dried hair and earring in place. The car is built like a tank. Pulsating music and horn bray in joyful disharmony. Young men in a hurry to go nowhere, young men screaming for attention. Their gleaming Mitsubishi Lancer is too big for Indian roads; it also has one headlight bashed in, a war wound that declares these young warriors mean business.

"Scum," Shiv says to himself. "Rich lumpens."

Though they couldn't have heard him, they assume he is mouthing a challenge. They probably prefer their victims to be women drivers, but for the moment he will do. Shiv sees a flash of jeering faces, hears a burst of drums as the music reaches a hysterical pitch; and the car abruptly cuts to the right so it is just a few inches before his. He steps on the brake as far as it will go. Other cars behind him begin honking.

Meanwhile the white car—its back an impenetrable wall, its antenna a swaying lance—is racing ahead. The boy at the back turns around to wave Shiv a derisive goodbye.

The shop Shiv finds after several inquiries is a hole in the wall, every inch of wall space covered with luridly colored gods and goddesses. Appropriately below the picture of the divine Lakshmi seated on a lotus is a sticker that declares: Corruption is National Menace. We Must Root Out Corruption in All Parameters of Activity. The shop owner, a plump, cheerful man, gestures grandly at his wares when Shiv tells him what he needs. Under the watchful eyes of the pantheon, Shiv looks at the crutches lined up against the wall. There are also calipered leg splints of all sizes, walkers that look like little enclosing gates, and even a couple of chairs with neat holes on their seats to make an Indian-style toilet more infirm-friendly.

Shiv selects a pair of light aluminum crutches and tries walking with them. The shopkeeper cheers him on, admiring his attempts at negotiating the patch of space between the rows of empty calipers, strapped and ready to be filled in.

As he puts the plastic-wrapped crutches in the car, Shiv notices a shop selling ice cream. On an impulse, he locks the car and goes into the shop. Rekha and he always buy old-fashioned vanilla, so he assumes Meena would like something different. Back in the car, he puts the bag with a brick of chocolate chip and another of Pistachio Paradise on the seat next to him. No encounter with lumpens this time; all the way home Shiv is stuck behind a truck with advice painted on its rear in cheerful colors. A big arrow points to the right; below it are the words RIGHT SIDE. To the left is another arrow, captioned with the cautionary word SUSIDE. The truck spews evil-looking and evil-smelling smoke, but it negotiates the narrow road at an exemplary sedate pace. Shiv raises the window glass, says goodbye to the petrol budget, and switches on the AC.

Meena is waiting for him in her small room, lying in bed, reading. Already this has become her room. What used to be Shiv's study table is now covered with her things: books, magazines, newspapers, clothes, a hairbrush, an alarm clock. The ceiling fan hums furiously.

Meena is transparently pleased to see him; Shiv finds something touching about this. Whatever she thinks or feels is there on Meena's face, not just faithfully mirrored, but multiplied in intensity—as if her face has captured the potent essence of every passing emotion. Kamla has given Meena her lunch and been to check on her twice. But she's bored, she's so bored; and the leg in the cast is itchy; and she feels dirty, she wants a proper bath.

Shiv switches on the cooler though it was drained of water several weeks back. There is a blast of warm air, then the cooler settles down to a deep bass drone, harmonizing with the ceiling fan.

He pulls the crutches out of the plastic bag and Meena tries them out. They are too tall for her. He fiddles with the screws and adjusts them so that they are just the right height for Meena. Shiv is amazed by his success; theirs is the sort of household where Rekha has to call an electrician to change a lightbulb.

Meena is like a child with several new toys—first the new crutches; then the tubelike plastic bag the crutches came in, perfect, she says, to cover the cast when bathing; and most of all, the chocolate chip ice cream. Then Shiv tells her he has applied for leave, and that he will be home to look after her.

The spoon that has been moving regularly between the bowl of ice cream and her mouth pauses. She looks up into his face through a long unruly curl that hangs over one eye. Even Meena's face, he sees, is capable of keeping a secret or two. But her look, though it is a look Shiv cannot read easily, convinces him. He can play guardian to Meena, his yet-to-be-discovered ward, at least for a few weeks.

THREE

AUGUST 25—SEPTEMBER 3

*T*hey are settling down to a routine, Meena, Kamla and Shiv. Meena's suitcase is unpacked; Shiv has persuaded her to give away the battered thing to Kamla. The narrow wooden cupboard in the study, which used to be stuffed with Shiv's files, now holds Meena's clothes. The telephone is by her bed. Shiv offered to move the music system into the room but Meena said there was no point; she claims to be tone-deaf. He moved the television set instead, though he notices her attention wanders as much as his does when they watch a couple of daytime tearjerkers.

Shiv has just one picture on his study wall—a simply framed photograph of the Hampi ruins in South India. In the foreground to the right is a wheel of stone, one of four wheels supporting a stone chariot. In the photograph only one wheel is visible. Shiv has never tired of looking at this wheel of enormous dimensions, standing still as if frozen for a moment before it begins to rotate again. In the background of the photograph looms a majestic hall, a rock-hewn elephant guarding its entrance. The hall is lined with rows of singing pillars—each pillar is reputed to sing a different note when struck. The pillars are decorated with exuberantly sculpted scenes from everyday life: street scenes, hunters, dancing girls.

The day Meena's roommate brought a plastic bag full of things from their hostel room, two new pictures went up on the wall. Posters, stuck on the wall with Sellotape, one on either side of the photograph of ruins. One of the pictures is a feminist poster of some sort; no words, just an image of matchstick women holding hands to make a perfect circle.

The other poster has a gray line drawing of a face of indeterminate gender in the background. On the face, smudgily printed in black, are the lines by the Reverend Martin Neimöller, the German pastor who spent eight years of his life in Nazi concentration camps:

In Germany they first came for the Communists,
and I didn't speak up because I wasn't a Communist.

Then they came for the Jews,
and I didn't speak up because I wasn't a Jew.

Then they came for the trade unionists,
and I didn't speak up because I wasn't a trade unionist.

Then they came for the Catholics,
and I didn't speak up because I was a Protestant.

Then they came for me—
and by that time no one was left to speak up.

At the top of the poster are the words in screaming red **Speak Up! Before It's Too Late.** Shiv reads this and feels a twinge of discomfort. But after all, he tells himself, Rekha is not around to disapprove; and it's just a couple of harmless posters, part of growing-up paraphernalia. He says nothing to Meena about his study's new political look.

Kamla has lost her look of virtuous suffering, having discovered how ferociously independent Meena is despite the cast. Now that she has no worries about extra work, or about juggling hours in all the houses she works in, Kamla is free to express human interest in the situation. She cooks a delicious meal once a day and washes dishes. She offers Babli after school hours to fetch and carry, or keep Meena company. And Shiv—for the first time in his life he makes breakfast for two; tea for two; snacks for two. He goes to markets he has not been to for years, unlikely shopping lists to hand. A white plastic stool for Meena to sit on while bathing. A showerhead and tube he attaches to the bathroom tap so that Meena does not have to bend for a bucket-bath. Girlish skirts because Meena cannot wear her shalwars and jeans. Ice cream, chocolates, fruit, even flowers. Meena approves of all the edible gifts but is indifferent to the flowers. She does not seem to notice when Shiv moves them to his room upstairs.

Meena is a sociology student; she is writing a thesis on what she calls women's stories, stories of women affected by the anti-Sikh riots after Indira Gandhi's assassination in 1984. She has finished doing the interviews—the fieldwork. Bedbound, this is the ideal time to begin putting it all together. Shiv tells her as much. "But how do you write in bed?" she says. "I am not even sure I can *think*, lying around like this all day." Instead they fill up the empty hours with games. A game of chess; he beats her easily. Then Scrabble. Cards. Shiv knows only two games, rummy and blackjack. Meena knows an astonishing number of card games, all learnt, she says, on long train journeys.

Shiv searches his daughter's cupboard for other relics of her childhood. At the back of a shelf he finds a dusty round wooden board, neat black lines on it like the latitude and longitude lines of the globe in a school atlas. With the board there is a box of little wooden animals: twelve white sheep, one yellow tiger, its mouth open, the paint on its tongue still startlingly red. He has never seen the game before. Perhaps Rekha or her mother played with it. He takes it down to Meena and they spend an evening making up different versions of a strategy game. When Shiv is the tiger, he is only allowed to move ahead one step a turn. Meena's sheep move in all directions, a step forward or backward, two steps diagonally. By the time it is Meena's turn to play tiger, they have altered the rules of the game; neither tiger nor sheep can move backward.

As Shiv puts away the animals in their box, he studies the tiger in his hand. Even though its face is crudely painted, it is expressive. The sheep faces are somewhat bland, but the wooden tiger looks hungry: single-minded. A little like Arya's new look.

But side by side with Arya's ugly bigoted face, Shiv remembers another, equally evocative one. The face of Arya's blind child, a face so oval and delicate that the vacant look about the eyes comes as a shock. Arya is completely devoted to this child. When Arya's eyes rest on his child's face, when his eyes brim with tenderness, where does his hatred go and hide? Shiv remembers Arya's wife saying to Rekha in one of the rare social gatherings of their Department, "Akshai's papa does everything for him. He won't even let me bathe the child." She looks both proud and pained as she says this; she laughs a strained, artificial laugh, a laugh she has to cough up like a foreign body stuck in her throat.

On an impulse Shiv tells Meena about the two Aryas, the Department-Arya and the father-Arya.

"You're trying your best to humanize him, aren't you," says Meena. "Why should we rack our brains figuring out his life? Finding out what made him such a twisted piece? He's like all his ancestors—tyrants capable of personal acts of kindness. Nazis who responded to music and poetry."

Meena listens intently when he tells her about Arya and the meeting. "I'm not surprised," she says. "They're crawling out of the woodwork now that it's their season." She looks at Shiv in the way she has, directly into his eyes, her chin cocked in a sideways, challenging stance. "You don't like confrontations, do you?"

It has been a week since Shiv went to a meeting. The Head's secretary must be back. He wonders, in passing, if there is an awkwardness in her now. A self-consciousness about being labeled a foreigner, a minority. A little fear, or at least discomfort, when she comes face to face with Arya. Shiv has been to the Department a couple of times, briefly, to see to work arrangements while on leave. But more and more the Department, the Head and his team, the entire B.A. History correspondence program—all are growing distant. As if they belong to a life already lived out, a life to be reflected on because over and done with. Or a life on hold. Though he works every day on the papers he has brought home with him, his real life now converges on a house with two people. A nurse and patient team: he is the nurse, Meena the patient.

Wherever Shiv is in the house, whatever he is doing, he is aware of another presence. The woman in the narrow bed in his study, a young woman. Almost a girl, except that she seems more worldly-wise sometimes than he. She talks of causes and street theater, *gender* and *courting arrest,* with the ease of a veteran. She too, he has discovered, is a frequenter of meetings, though her meetings are played out in a world where a different language is spoken—where it is possible to feel passions foreign to him. Though she lies in bed, her leg encased in fiberglass, she does not seem aware of her powerlessness.

And though she has been in his house for just a week, already there is a minor conspiracy of silence they have become partners in. Or not quite partners; it was she who decided her parents should not be told about the broken knee. Or about his playing guardian for the first time. Or about their being alone together.

Sometimes, when he sees Meena in her bright yellow T-shirt, the polished brown face framed by the halo of tangled hair, Shiv thinks of her mother, his childhood neighbor Sumati. He has forgotten what Sumati looks like as an adult. What he remembers of her, or what her daughter summons with an occasional raising of her well-defined chin, is the picture of a playmate. A summer playmate of two or three years' standing, a girl with untidy curls escaping her two plaits, shrill-voiced, mocking. A swift runner. The kind who does something to you, and before you have registered your hurt or indignity, takes to her feet. Shiv knows nothing about his old friend's life now, about her tussles with less unsuspecting playmates, her success with hit-and-run tactics. It is her daughter who has now been hurt; and for the time being she cannot run.

The next morning Kamla does not come down to cook. She sends Babli to say that she has a fever. Shiv goes up the winding stairs once again. Kamla is in bed, fast asleep. Babli has not gone to school. She comes to the door, looking important, and takes the strip of aspirin he has brought. She whispers, "I'll look after her, Sahib. My father will come clean the house before he leaves for work. And I will sit by Didi when you have to go out."

Shiv gives her cheek a gentle pinch and looks at Kamla's flushed face on the mattress laid out on the floor. He hesitates, but two patients are beyond his newfound nursing abilities. As it is, he will have to cook for Meena and himself till Kamla is better.

Meena is amused by his look of dismay. "I'll help you," she says like Babli. "It should be no problem."

"But do you know how to cook?"

"I've never tried, but so what? You drive, I'll navigate," she says breezily.

She limps with her crutches to the dining table and sits down, the leg in the cast stretched out, the foot resting on a stool. For a novice, she is surprisingly competent with a knife. Shiv watches entranced as her fingers disappear in a blur of swift, coordinated movement. The onions collapse on the board in a cascade of slivers. Then cabbage, beans, garlic, ginger. He tosses the vegetables—inexpertly, some of them escaping the pan—in a spoonful of hot oil and mixes it all with the rice he has cooked. Lunch has a festive feel to it; they bask jointly in a glow of achievement. Then Shiv remembers he will have to do it all over again at dinnertime, and that blunts the triumph a little.

At night, reading in bed upstairs, Shiv hears Meena's bell. She no longer calls him professor—to his relief. Also to his relief, she does not call him the ubiquitous *Uncle,* an address he has grown to loathe. For the present, he remains her nameless companion.

He goes down and finds her sitting up in bed. Though the fan in the cooler is on full blast, her face is damp with sweat. "I can't sleep," she says. "I'm so restless."

"What about a game of cards? Or chess?"

"I'm sick of games. Just sit here and talk to me."

"What about a drink?" Shiv asks. She agrees to a rum. He pours her a small one and a large whisky for himself. He sits down on the chair by her bed.

He looks at the papers lying on the bed by her. She picks them up and stacks them in a pile on the table. He passes her a paperweight, an odd-shaped round stone he picked up outside the ruins of Hampi.

"How did you manage your interviews?" he asks Meena, gesturing at the pile of handwritten sheets. "Was it difficult getting the women to talk to you?"

"It was. For the first week, I thought it was going to be impossible. I went with a friend who speaks fluent Punjabi and I thought that would help. But the women were tired and suspicious." Meena breaks off, takes a little gulp of her rum, and continues. "They were tired of telling their stories to all kinds of people who came and asked them painful questions, then went away never to be seen again. Suspicious, because they knew by now that their stories were going to be used by people. Twisted by different groups to suit their own purposes."

"Then? How did you get them to believe you were different?"

"It wasn't me. It was one of them, a young woman who had lost her husband and her father. She was a few months pregnant when they were killed; she miscarried a week later. It was she who said, 'Behen, I'll help you. I don't know what you will do with your tape of our stories. What use our empty lives will be to you in your studies. But I have lost so much—I have nothing left in my stomach but anger. I also have a hunger that says, tell your story, tell it again and again to whoever will listen.' It was she, young Jasbir Kaur, who convinced the others that they should talk to me."

"Courage is a strange thing, isn't it?" Shiv says, watching Meena grimace at what is left of her drink.

She looks at him questioningly as if she has not heard him right.

"Not just courage, but also anger, passion—the combination of all three I should say. I was thinking of my father." Shiv takes a deep swallow of his whisky. "He was a freedom fighter, but for him the freedom movement didn't end in 1947. In fact, the burdens of the new world—the travails of a free India—sat heavy on his shoulders."

Shiv pauses; Meena waits for him to go on. "He disappeared," Shiv says, standing up and taking her empty glass. "He was the bravest man I knew, but still he couldn't keep it up; it must have finally broken him. He went to Indore for a meeting of Congress workers and sent a telegram home about the date of his return train journey. Later my uncle found his name on the passenger list. But he didn't come home to Coimbatore; the ticket officer said a man was in the third-class seat—seat 16A—for the first part of the journey. Someone in the same compartment said he got off at a small station."

"Did you hear from him again?" Meena asks, her eyes soft with sympathy.

"No. There were the usual newspaper advertisements. My uncle tried everything he could think of, made the journey to Indore and back several times looking for information. My mother spent the rest of her life performing all sorts of pujas to lead him back to us. But nothing—we never heard of him again."

Shiv brings back freshly filled glasses and they sit listening to the duet of the fan and cooler. Though they drink in silence, the little room is snug. It holds the two of them in a cocoon of companionable sympathy. Or if not sympathy, understanding; of what is not easily said; of what is best left unsaid.

It is very late into the night when he says goodnight to Meena—still sober, a young woman who knows how to hold her liquor. He wishes he were half as sure of himself. He bends over her and straightens the covers. Then he gently pushes into place a strand of hair falling across her cheek. She smiles, a mysterious, sleepy smile. His fingertips take away with them a touch of her warm, moist cheek.

But it is a different softness that seeps into Shiv's dreams that night, the soft residue of some old, blurred images. The rocking motion of a bullock cart. His father's hand holding his, his father's hand not as soft as his mother's. His father's booming voice, used to shouting slogans for freedom, exhorting his countrymen to resist colonial rule, fills the cart. The cart smells of bullocks. One of the bullocks, the long-tailed one, shudders over a bump in the road and they sway as if they are in a boat being tossed about in a storm. The cow lifts its tail and shoots an arc of pee into the wind. He squeals in delight and tugs at his father's arm. His father turns to him and smiles. The smile hangs in the air teasingly, then fades. His father is gone. Now he is watching his mother light the kitchen fire. (But he was older when his father disappeared, why is he such a little boy here? And why does she wear a happy face instead of her usual grieving one?)

Early morning light, pale, a reluctant blue, gently dripping down the mean little skylight. His barefoot mother, slim, compact, on her haunches before the mound of ash and kindling sticks. Her soft muttering monotone of prayer, as if she is humming without knowing it. The sound of the iron rod in her hand scraping, spreading out the ash and the charred lumps from the day before. Then the humming goes away. She bends forward, her face close enough to the stove to whisper secrets. She blows. Exhales like wind, almost whistling as she speaks to the fire in the only language it knows. Then she gets up, goes out to get wood. He tiptoes to the stove and peers into the little pit. The vessel-shaped cave. The cave looks back at him. Its mouth is full of hard, glittering red eyes. They wink at him before his mother returns and pulls him away.

Shiv woke up at his usual hour, refreshed despite his whisky-induced dreams. Meena slept late into the morning; Shiv's guess is that she would still be sleeping if the fan had not come to a standstill. He has not seen Babli all morning. The house is silent, weighed down with its burden of sullen, humid air.

Meena moves her fingers through her long, messy hair. Every now and then her fingers meet an obstructing tangle. She frowns, tugs at the knot till it gives way. Her conquering fingers move ahead, down the length of her hair; then begin all over again, from the top, with another thick and rebellious strand.

Perhaps, in her whole life, this might be the time she is most beautiful. Shiv thinks this and she holds out a strand of hair before her, squints at it disapprovingly and asks him, "Will you help me wash my hair? I could sit on a chair and lean back over the bathroom sink."

Shiv feels like a priest at a ritual. He places a plastic chair in front of the sink, a stool by it. On the stool, a bottle of shampoo, a towel, and the head of the handheld shower he has improvised for Meena. He takes Meena's crutches from her and helps her to sit as comfortably as she can on the chair. The leg in the cast stretches out before her like a shapely log of white wood. Meena examines the shampoo bottle—which he has brought down from Rekha's cupboard—and grins wickedly. It's called, Shiv now notices with some embarrassment, Femme Fatale.

Meena leans back, lets her hair fall into the sink like a dark curtain. Shiv places the showerhead in the sink and connects the tube to a tap, then runs the water. The water is cool and refreshing; she shuts her eyes as he moves the shower around her head. He has some trouble opening the bottle of Femme Fatale but he finally manages to squeeze too much of it onto the palm of his hand. The bathroom fills with a potent fragrance. Meena, her eyes still shut, sniffs. "Very fancy," she murmurs, "I won't know myself."

This is becoming a game, a better game than rummy or tiger-and-sheep. Shiv smears the shampoo over her head, then massages her scalp with it. She exhales. He works the lather down the length of her hair. The rinsing is not so easy; he splashes himself and gets her neck and T-shirt wet. His eyes dart to the stiff nipples visible under her T-shirt, then back to her hair, half-ashamed. When she straightens her dripping head, she leaves behind an unhappy gray puddle of grit in the sink. For some reason he is grateful she cannot see this. She leans back again and he rinses her hair once more. It is now a heavy thing in his hands, glossy and alive in the filtered light coming in through the bathroom window.

Later, sitting on his chair in the study, her leg resting on the bed, Meena towels her hair dry. Her face glows. Her face, Shiv thinks, must always be animated. But it wears now a look of inward absorption—similar to her look when she is eating a bowl of chocolate ice cream. A look of concentration, as if firmly focusing on something within reach.

He stands there, watching her, unwilling to let go of his priestly role. She seems to sense this. Almost magnanimously she passes the hairbrush to him. Wordlessly he goes to work at the tangles, the headily fragrant masses of wet hair, a craftsman before his half-finished masterpiece.

Meena in a T-shirt the color of grapes. A white skirt that deepens the brown of her bare right leg. Her washed, combed hair held back neatly with a fat velvety rubber band. A pair of silver earrings shaped like raindrops hang from her ears. She is sitting up in bed eagerly awaiting her friends who have rung up to get Shiv's address.

Two boys and a girl. (Or, Shiv corrects himself, two young men and one young woman.) One of the boys, a tall, unshaven one, shakes hands with Shiv, taking in the man and the house

in a quick, sweeping glance. "I am Amar," he says. "This is
Jyoti, this is Manzar." The two nod at Shiv unsmilingly.

Meena calls out impatiently, "Hi—I'm here—come on!"
Shiv follows them to Meena's room; they embrace her one after
the other. Amar sits on the bed; Jyoti on the chair.

"Shall I get another chair?" Shiv asks. "And tea or something cold?"

"No," says Meena, her eyes shining. "Just shut the door,
please. So our noise won't disturb you," she adds as an afterthought.

Outside the shut door, in the instant before he moves away,
Shiv hears Meena's voice say, "Tell me what's been happening.
I'm bored out of my mind."

Shiv goes upstairs, resolving not to come down till he gets some
work done. His desk looks at him reproachfully. It is weighed
down with neat piles of lessons, letters, syllabi, and half-read
assignments. Holiday homework. A full new lesson to be written, a lesson on the rise and fall of the medieval Vijayanagar
empire. It was some years ago he visited the ruins of this
empire—the Hampi ruins, now a World Heritage site in the
state of Karnataka. He has all the notes ready on his desk, both
from the usual texts and his own journal of the trip. He is, for
once, looking forward to writing a new lesson. He has assigned
this particular one to himself as something of a treat.

The grandeur of Vijayanagar persists even in its ruins. The
palaces and temples and fortification walls in Hampi dwarfed
Shiv, just as they must have amazed and diminished its citizens hundreds of years ago. He looked at all this evidence of
might—might laid waste—and was struck afresh by how small
a thing a single life is. How small, how trivial and fragile, with-

out the weighty anchoring of the past. But it is all too easy to look at the Hampi ruins and fashion only two images of the past. One as a testimonial to imperial grandeur, the other as a testimonial to the human capacity for destruction. Surely the past is more than a mere fossil? Or a perfect cast whose mold has been broken? Shiv feels a sudden rush of ambition: he would like to write a lesson that weeds out stereotypes, makes realistic assessments. To take this fragment from the medieval past and reconstruct an entire range of possibilities.

Simple challenge, big challenge. The kind Shiv's father would have echoed with approval. "Shiv," he can hear his father's ghost say to him now, "if you want to get hold of something and learn all about it, *know* it, it doesn't matter whether that something is in the past or the present. All that matters is that you are freethinking. That you have moral courage."

This should inspire Shiv to put pen to paper immediately, but instead his mind drifts to Arya and his band of pirates, looters of the past. He puts his pen down; he catches himself listening for sounds from downstairs. Is that the front door being opened then shut? Meena may be alone again. She may need him. Shiv pushes back his chair, stands up. The desk, and its burden of history, can wait another hour or two.

FOUR

SEPTEMBER 4–6

Shiv opens the door and peeps into his study, setting of gloomy thoughts and prosaic history. But *this* room has opened its arms to the light. To the dazzling summer sky. How did the sun get into his study? A shiny, ripe piece of sunshine?

The day after Meena's friends visit her, she has to see the doctor for the first time since her leg was put in plaster. By the time Shiv goes down to her room in the morning, she is already up, dressed and ready to go. She is wearing a long skirt, a modest brown. She has one shoe on. Her hair is knotted in a fat coil at the back of her neck. She could be a girl impatient to go to a long-awaited party, her face bright with anticipation, her shoulder bag on the bed by her.

"I've been so revoltingly good," she says to Shiv. "I've rested the leg exactly as the doctor said, for two whole weeks. Do you think he will take off the cast next week?"

Virtue is always rewarded. This lesson learnt in childhood persists, turning into a comforting superstition when other infantile certainties are left behind. What can Shiv say to Meena when she looks at him with such hope? With such appeal in her eyes, as if he can persuade the doctor to set her free? But he is saved from mouthing cautionary platitudes. A sudden noise cuts him off, a crash in the living room where Kamla's husband is dusting, sweeping and swabbing all at once.

Kamla's husband is one of those men who seem to have been created only to prove that appearances are deceptive. He has the graceful, elegant body of a dancer. His features are borrowed from an exquisite, romantic miniature painting. But there is a bull lurking in this pretty picture. If a thing is breakable, he will break it. If it cannot break, he will spill it, tear it, dent it. By the time Kamla is well, Rekha's arty objects and copper-bottomed pans will probably look like survivors of a domestic genocide.

Now, in the living room, Shiv sees that the latest victim is the telephone. Kamla's husband picks it up and eagerly shows it to Shiv so that he can see it is not broken. Shiv takes the receiver and puts it to his ear; the dial tone is gone.

"It's dead," Shiv snaps at Kamla's husband. "What have you done?"

Kamla's husband stares at Shiv, his slanting, thick-lashed eyes full of reproach; then he blinks, falls to his knees and picks up the wires. This drives Shiv frantic. He knows that when Kamla's husband fixes anything, the result is invariably more dramatic than when he cleans it.

Meena has followed Shiv to the living room on her crutches. Kamla's husband lets go of the wires and stands up, his face filling with an infuriating meek innocence. "Never mind," Meena says to Shiv, "we'll be late if we don't leave soon. The extension in my room is working anyway. Why do you need so many phones?"

Shiv is not sure if Kamla's husband has understood what Meena said, but he smiles at her to say that *she* understands, *her* priorities are right. He flicks his duster one last time at the dead telephone. "I'll repair it when I return," he promises, and picks up his duster, broom and bucket. Shiv notices that the filthy, dripping swab cloth has shed several stringy edges. They lie on the freshly swept floor like coiled gray worms.

Outside the house Meena halts, takes a deep breath and looks around as if seeing the world for the first time. Shiv waits for her to look her fill before taking the crutches from her. Seen through her eyes, the familiar campus acquires vast and mysterious dimensions. Was its skyline always so bare and awesome, were the buildings always so forbiddingly opaque, enclosing unfathomable secrets? The bougainvillea bush across the driveway blazes purple sunlight.

Getting into the car quickly cures Meena of sentiment and benevolence. "Shit," she mutters, her teeth clenched as she slides herself onto the backseat and Shiv shuts the door. The glass on the windows has to be raised so she can lean against one window and flex her feet against the other.

Shiv gets in, looks at her to see if she is all right. Her forehead and upper lip glisten. "Do you want the AC?" he asks her, pulling out his handkerchief. She shakes her head and takes the handkerchief from him.

The hospital is a newly constructed building separated from the outside world by an impeccable crewcut lawn. The potted plants along the driveway stand at attention as if they wear stiffly starched uniforms. On either side of the hospital, there are empty lots piled high with garbage and construction rubble. Shiv drives past a large sign with a stern warning: No Outside Food Allowed. Beyond, to the side of the building, he parks near a ramp for patients with wheelchairs.

Meena refuses to wait in the car; "I am getting squashed," she says. "Help me to get out of here." But she finds it difficult to maneuver the crutches up the ramp. Shiv hurries inside to find a wheelchair. It is only when the wheelchair and attendant arrive that they realize Meena cannot sit with both feet on the chair's footrest. The attendant moves to pick up the leg in the cast. Shiv hastens forward; he can't bear the thought that the attendant may not be gentle enough. Equally, he can't bear seeing a stranger touch Meena's cast. Shiv asks the attendant to push the wheelchair instead; Meena balances the leg in the cast midair; and Shiv heads their little parade, holding Meena's leg, walking backward into the waiting room.

The air is a delicate mixture of phenol and incense. One of the walls in the waiting room has a large glass-covered cup-board. Ganesha, by virtue of being Remover of Obstacles, sits imprisoned inside, his trunk resting limply on his rotund belly. He looks on without comment as Shiv pays for the X ray and consultation in advance. Armed with all the receipts, they head for the X-ray room.

Shiv and a nurse help Meena onto the X-ray table. Shiv can see that Meena is in pain but she does not say a thing. The firm set of her mouth and her clammy hands overwhelm him with a protective feeling, a feeling that is entirely superfluous, considering it has nowhere to go.

An hour later they are in the doctor's room; he holds Meena's X ray up to the light. "Looks alright," he says, and Meena perks up immediately.

"When do I get rid of the cast?" she asks him, leaning on her elbows to sit up.

"Oh, the cast," he says, and the telephone rings. For the next five minutes he grunts a series of h'ms, yes's and noes into the phone, his monosyllabic version of the doctor's bedside manner. His pen traces elaborate doodles on the pad before him.

"The cast, Doctor," Meena says the instant he puts down the phone. "You said it would be off in three to four weeks. Three weeks if I was careful about resting the leg."

"It's been just over two weeks now."

"Yes, but you said the X ray was alright."

"It's healing—you don't want to interfere with that. You can put both feet on the ground and use just one crutch. Or use a walker."

"But for how long," begins persistent Meena.

"Let's see—you could get an X ray and a checkup in another five weeks or so."

"Five more?" gasps Meena and the telephone rings again. The doctor covers the mouth of the receiver with his hand and says, "I'll see you then." His lips stretch in imitation of a smile and he returns to his telephone. His head bends over the doodle pad.

Boredom. Yet another power cut. Meena is restless and sullen. She complains that her knee is itchy. Halfway down the cast, it is impossible to reach. But she refuses to give up; she has, by now, an imaginative range of what she calls scratchers. A sharp letter opener; a discarded comb; a long white-ribbed peacock feather; an incense stick. She keeps these in a brass jug on the table by her bed. Every now and then Shiv sees her inserting one of the scratchers into her cast, her skirt bunched up at the top of her thigh. Her face has, at these moments, the concentration of a predator, entirely without inhibition or self-consciousness. Once, when she sees him watching, she complains that the cast is chafing her ankle. He follows her instructions. His finger dripping with cream, he traces circles round her ankle over and over again. The raw skin gleams once he has drawn this slippery anklet. Then he rolls bits of cotton into small balls and pushes them into the lower end of the cast.

But it is not always so easy to distract her. If Rekha were here, she would have known how to fill up the empty minutes with bright, purposeful small talk. But she is not here—and Shiv is not sorry the task of amusing Meena is entirely his. Keep the conversation light, he tells himself as if lecturing an earnest student. Keep it playful, skim over all the boring puddles like a dragonfly. Tell her stories, entertaining anecdotes. Meena loves it when the butt of the joke is what she calls the cardboard tyrants: the university authorities, the management, the senior faculty. And god knows there are enough clowns among them; Shiv sacrifices them without a qualm. He racks his brains for a new story.

"Did I tell you about the Admin Officer and the gender petition?" (Shiv is terrified he may repeat a story and lose his audience of one.)

"No." Meena yawns, then covers her mouth with her hand like an afterthought. She looks at him expectantly.

"A group of women employees took a petition against gender discrimination to the Officer. Okay, he said to them, show me your gender thing. Oh no—you show us yours first, said the women."

Meena's eyes sparkle; Shiv is getting addicted to this sparkle. University folklore converted into stories with punchlines. Childish games with words: rector as rectum, adult education as adultery education. Shiv is taking a crash course from Meena on how to live with power and not give up laughter. Survival by play; play as survival mode. Words, more words. What else can connect them? A passing touch, an accidental meeting of his fingertips, her skin, when he settles the cushion under her foot. He knows every inch of the cast that takes the shape of her leg.

"Will you get me something to read?" she asks him.

He eyes the pile of pamphlets her friend Amar has left on the table. "Oh, I've read those, they're not exactly absorbing," she says airily. "I've read half of *Orientalism* and the book is in the hostel. Could you get me a copy? And wait—" She searches under the mess of sheets and pillows and finds something else she has been reading. Asterix, Obelix and Co. "Will you get me some of these?" she asks a little sheepishly. "Especially *Asterix and the Normans*—I haven't read that."

He bounces up and out, charged with energy and purpose as if she has asked him to get her the moon. He buys her Edward Said and a pile of Asterix, and for good measure, Tintin as well. But this is apparently a mistake. "Tintin is nothing like Asterix," she says, no longer sheepish about her closet comic-habit. "It's shamelessly imperialist."

He promises to return the Tintin immediately.

"And if you're going out, will you get me batteries for the emergency light?" (He has been insisting she keep this by her bed in case the power fails at night.) "Oh, but don't get batteries made by those murderers Union Carbide."

When Shiv returns with the approved batteries and the generally approved flavor of ice cream, Meena is in the bathroom. It takes her half an hour to have an unsatisfactory shower with her cast in a plastic bag held in place with a piece of string. He puts away what he has bought and uses this time to make her bed. The sheets are damp. There are two dead mosquitoes on one pillow, and a bloodstain shaped like a teardrop. He straightens the sheets, dusts them down top to bottom with the pillow. (Rekha will never believe he has done this instead of Kamla.) Before he returns the pillow to the bed and covers it with the bedspread, he pauses for a minute, looking at the lumpy, leaky pillow in his hand. He buries his face in it. The pillowcase does not smell fresh. It is not exactly unpleasant either; it smells warm, human, of hot cheeks and thick damp hair. He breathes in, holds the smell. He fills a bottle in his brain with this perfume, a nameless essence. Then he traps it, hoards it, and holds it in with a tight-fitting stopper.

The morning begins with "loadshedding" for an hour, then a "breakdown" for two. By the time the power finally returns, Meena has gone back to sleep. Kamla too has returned to work, though she looks too washed out to do much. Shiv settles down with his neglected papers upstairs. Amita Sen has called to say that she has to send a course module to the printing unit. He is to read it, approve it and send it back to her. Then with careful politeness, she asks how his ward is; she does not ask when he is returning to the Department.

Amita's module begins with the obligatory Lesson Objective; Shiv has trained her himself to follow this safe structure familiar to their students. *After reading this lesson you will be able to . . .* In this case, it is drawing links between the major religions of India and social reform movements.

As if a button has been pressed, a part of Shiv is on the alert as he reads on. Though he has never said as much, the Head pushed for Shiv's being In-Charge of B.A. History because he was sure that Shiv would, while being liberal, "balance any Marxist bias." The Head's great fear is that the "consensus approach" so dear to his heart may be demolished by some course expert who is "too controversial" or "dominating" or "given to extreme ideas."

The real danger they face is that they put their lectures down in print. Unlike regular teachers, they never get a chance to correct or qualify what has already been said in an earlier class. Shiv remembers all the indignant letters of protest they got some years ago when two little illustrations got past the course editor. One was a line drawing of a congregation of Muslim faithful bent in prayer, all the bent figures facing exactly the opposite of the prescribed west. Even worse, the second line drawing attempted to illustrate polygamy: the drawing had a graybeard reminiscent of some venerable old mullah in the center, surrounded by four women pulling him in four different directions.

But Amita's module is bland and beyond reproach. Shiv puts it aside and goes on to the next lot of papers, all part of a course on the Far East. His attention wanders; he wonders what Meena would make of the Head; of Amita; of their entire troupe of module-peddlers.

Meena. Fish-eyed. Fish-eyed, dark-browed, tangle-haired.

Wide-hipped, generous-lipped. The list he can chant seems endless. Shiv invokes Meena, Meena's attributes, with a thousand names—like a devotee who mumbles himself into a stupor. A devotee whose words keep him upstairs in safety, while the flesh and blood reality lies downstairs in her room. The room. Such dignifying of that small space, a glorified hole, to call it a room. Meena must feel she is sleeping in a cupboard, marking time while lying prone on a shelf. She is too young to appreciate such compact safety, the comfort of being held in and enclosed.

Shiv turns back to his work, resolute. By the afternoon he has taken care of all the papers on his desk except for the new lesson. He gets up, tired and virtuous, and goes downstairs. He makes his way to Meena's room.

Shiv and Meena sit in the stream of late afternoon light filtered by the mosquito mesh on her window. Shiv has drawn the curtain halfway across so that the sun does not get in Meena's eyes. The TV is on. Meena has been yawning her way through the third B-grade detective film she has seen this week. Shiv's contribution to her enjoyment sits on a tray she balances on her lap. A cup of tea, the chocolate bourbon biscuits she is partial to, a bowl of tangy masala peanuts.

The detective has just discovered that he has been double-crossed by his love interest, a blonde with a fictitious Barbie-doll figure. There is a sense that this betrayal will speed up the film; the decisive chase and shootout are just minutes away. Just then the telephone by Meena's bed rings shrilly. Shiv picks it up. Meena reaches for the remote and lowers the volume. The detective plays out his inevitable triumph over the baddies in silence.

A young man whose name Shiv doesn't catch is on the phone, asking for the "professor sir." The man introduces himself as a reporter of a newspaper called *Current*.

"Professor? Professor Shiv Murthy? Can you confirm that you are on leave?"

"Yes," says Shiv, "but how would that interest your paper?"

"Sir—professor—I want to meet you for an interview. About your controversial article."

"What article? I'm sorry, I don't know what you are talking about."

"Sir, are you saying 'No comment'? Don't you want to present your side of the story?"

"I would, if you would only tell me what the story is." Shiv swallows his exasperation. "Are you sure you have the right person? I teach in the History Department of the Central University. KGU. I can't remember when I last wrote an article in a newspaper or magazine."

"Sir." (The way he uses the word tells Shiv how completely he disbelieves him.) "I am talking about your article—or maybe you call it textbook or course or something—on some poet—wait a minute, please, sir, I have it here. Oh yes," he says, and reads from his notes. "It's an article on the twelfth-century poet and social reformer Basavanna. And you have yourself confirmed that you are on leave. Are you denying that you went on leave because of the protests against the article, sir?"

Shiv remains silent, trying to take it in; but none of it makes any sense yet.

"Sir? Are you still there? Did the university ask you to go on leave or is it voluntary?"

"My leave? I'm sorry, I can't talk to you till I have found out what this is all about."

"Not even a short interview on the telephone, sir?"

"No."

"No comment, sir?"

Shiv hangs up.

Meena has put aside her tray midway through Shiv's conversation with the alleged journalist. She is no longer yawning. "What is it," she asks eagerly. "What's happened?"

"I don't really know. Somebody from a paper called *Current* asking for an interview. Have you heard of this paper?"

"No, but what do they want to interview you about?"

"That's the strange part. This man seems to think I have gone on leave because of something I wrote—because there have been protests against it. He said something about Basavanna. I *have* written a course module on social reform movements in medieval India, where there is a lesson on Basava—usually referred to as Basavanna or Elder Brother Basava—but why would anyone protest about that?"

They sit in puzzled silence, then Meena says, "Why don't you find out what it's about? Suppose it's true and someone else calls? What if your Arya is up to something? You should know what's been happening while you have been on leave."

Shiv considers this. He supposes he should call Menon or Amita—just in case this is not some kind of sophisticated crank call. But how would a crank caller know his name? Or that he has written a history lesson for B.A. correspondence students on Basava?

The telephone rings again. Shiv looks at Meena, then picks it up with some trepidation. It's the Head.

"Shiv?" This use of his first name is so out of character that Shiv immediately knows something is wrong.

"Yes, Dr. Sharma," he forces himself to say. "How are you?"

"I'm fine, Shiv. Look, let me get to the point. I don't know if you are aware of it, but there is a problem with your medieval Indian history lessons."

"Yes, I had a peculiar phone call from someone claiming to be a journalist. He wanted to know why I am on leave. What seems to be the problem?"

"Your lesson on Basavanna's movement for social reform has been leaked somehow to the press."

"But Dr. Sharma," Shiv interrupts, "our lessons are hardly classified information. Anyone can get hold of them, in a library or in one of our study centers."

"I know, I know. But this time it's fallen into the wrong hands. It's a pity you didn't guard against ambiguity, Shiv. Apparently there is a certain lack of clarity in the lesson—anyway the lesson has hurt the sentiments of a Hindu watchdog group. You know our policy is to steer clear of controversy."

Meena leans forward, her face attentive, though she can hear only one end of the conversation. Shiv waits for the Head to catch his breath and go on.

"The Dean and I have received an angry, abusive letter about this lesson. I told the Dean I had not read the lesson myself since you are in charge of the B.A. program. This group, something called the Itihas Suraksha Manch, accuses you of distorting history and historical figures."

"Distorting history?" Shiv asks like a stupid echo.

The Head ignores his interruption. "It seems you have implied that Basavanna's city, Kalyana, was not a model Hindu kingdom. It seems you have exaggerated the problem of caste and written in a very biased way about the brahmins and temple priests. And also you have not made it clear enough that Basa-vanna was much more than an ordinary human being. There are people who consider him divine, you know."

"And my leave? What has that got to do with it?" Shiv asks, though he is beginning to discern a mad logic in the instant web being woven around him.

"Yes, we will have to decide what to do about that. There is a rumor that you have gone on leave because the lesson has got you into trouble."

"Dr. Sharma, I didn't know I was in trouble, as you put it, till five minutes ago."

"Well, Shiv, we will have to act swiftly to stop this from growing into a controversy. A full apology or retraction from you will be best—we can decide what to call it so that it is not too embarrassing for the Department—or for you of course. And we may have to send instructions to all our study centers to discontinue use of the booklet that contains this module. Maybe we will have to decide to reprint without the lesson. I have to meet the Dean tomorrow morning at eleven-thirty and give him a report. Please meet me before that—wait, I just remembered something else—maybe it's best we meet in the Dean's room. And get hold of a copy of the lesson by then if you don't have one at home."

Shiv can do nothing but agree, he is so bewildered by it all. He thinks of his careful vetting of Amita's module this morning; a morning so far back in time that he can hardly believe he planned to tell the story of the polygamy line drawing to entertain Meena.

Meena breaks into his confused thoughts and goes, in her special way, straight to the heart of the matter. "It's Arya, isn't it?"

"I don't know, but some crazy group has got hold of a lesson I wrote for the medieval history course. As far as I have understood, they are objecting to the fact that I have not made the heroes heroic enough, and that I have made the villains too villainous. At any rate, they claim the lesson *distorts* history." (Shiv mimes quotation marks to enclose the word.) "It seems I have not sung enough of a paean to the glory of Hindu kingdoms; and that I make too much of caste divisions among Hindus." Shiv frowns at the TV; the silent screen fills with madly celebrating village folk advertising their discovery of Coke. He takes the remote from Meena and switches it off. "The group is called the Itihas Suraksha Manch. The protection of history! Whoever heard of history having to be protected?"

"Protect?" says Meena with a knowing sneer. "The minute they use the word you know they mean attack."

Shiv considers this for a moment. It sounds a little shrill to him, and far too neat, but—it is true that whether people are talking about culture or history or women's rights, *protection* has become a much-abused word. A cover-up for all kinds of bullying tactics.

But Meena is a step or two ahead of Shiv. "What are you going to say tomorrow? You will have to chalk out a plan. Obviously you can't apologize or take back a word of the lesson."

Shiv's heart sinks. Is it all so obvious? He feels his eloquence about the complexities of history drying up at the thought of confronting fists, threats, physical danger in any form at all.

The telephone rings again. He picks it up in a daze. Nothing will surprise him, not even a call from the Dean asking for his resignation.

But it is Rekha. "Shiv? You haven't called for a while. Is everything alright?"

"Yes, of course, I was planning to call you tonight. I'll call you back later." For some reason, he feels uncomfortable talking to Rekha while Meena sits a foot away. The other two calls did not bring home the fact that only the telephone next to Meena's bed is working.

"Do that, but now that I've called, I had better tell you—I don't know if the gardener has been coming regularly, and I'm worried about my plants. I don't want everything drying up by the time I get back. I have a list for you—Shiv, are you listening? Will you get a pencil and jot this down?"

"Okay, go on," he says though he does not make a move to get a pencil or paper. He catches something about bamboo, Night Queen and heliconia. When she is finished, she says, "Have you got all that? Shiv—you haven't asked about Tara and her new job."

"How is she," he asks like a dutiful zombie.

"She's fine, she loves the job. You should see the size of your daughter's new office! But are you managing? You don't sound too well."

"I'm fine—really. Oh yes, Meena—Sumati's daughter Meena—is here for a few days. She's hurt her leg. No, it's nothing to worry about. Kamla is looking after her."

Shiv hangs up, steals a look at Meena to see how she has reacted to what she has heard. But this call—or his end of it— seems of no interest to her. The minute he hangs up, she says as if they were not interrupted, "What's the plan of action? How do we beat your fundoos at their game?"

Fundoos. How familiar Meena's generation is with the word *fundamentalist.* So much a fact of life that a nickname, *fundoos,* rolls off Meena's tongue with ease. A nickname for a pet, a pet enemy. The familiar garden-variety hatemonger, inescapable because he has taken root in your own backyard. Fundoo, fundamentalist. Fascist. Obscurantist. Terrorist. And the made-in-India brand, the communalist—a deceptively innocuous-sounding name for professional other-community haters.

Meena is waiting for Shiv, her head full of plans. To her it is a foregone conclusion that he will pick up a spear and a shield and rush headlong into battle. The new lesson waits upstairs to be written, the lesson that traces the fall of a wonder-city. Vijayanagar City waits to be sacked again, this time of its half-revealed memories. And as for Shiv—he has escaped both to sit idle in Rekha's garden, among her ambitious attempts to grow a lush landscape, complete with orchids on tree trunks, on Delhi's inhospitable rocky soil. The bamboo is to his right; he has identified this, the lantana hedge that needs shaping, the chikoo sapling, and the infant jasmines. It's the more intimidating names he has yet to put a plant to: Juniper horizontalis, heliconia, Ficus benjamina.

Rekha is good at naming things. To Shiv the garden is just so much soothing but undifferentiated greenery. When they first moved to this house, the backyard was a jungle of thorny shrubs and weeds, the kind that spread like an army advancing forward day by day. Rekha was dismayed, but Shiv could tell she was also excited by the challenge. He saw a look on her face that he imagines many of the conquerors of Delhi have shared; a gleam that assesses the strength of the enemy, and the spoils to be won. The kind of hungry look that wants to colonize as far as the eye can see, to clear and rearrange spaces and lives.

The men Rekha hired for daily wages cut and slashed,

chopped and dug. By the time they spread the manure-rich soil that came in odorous, tightly packed bags, the weedy army was a distant memory. The stretch of soil enclosed by barbed wire had the cowed look of an obedient subject. All the conqueror had to do was keep it domesticated—plant afresh on the blank tablet things of her choosing, things she could name and that depended on her for their survival.

Like Rekha, Meena names things with ferocious certainty. Communalist, fundamentalist. These women warriors seem to know exactly which cities they want to raze to the ground, which they want to raise in their place.

Shiv's own campaigns are minor rebellions, secretive mutinies. He is not used to keeping much back from Rekha. Sometimes he wonders if that is the real attraction Amita Sen holds for him. That if he has a few secret moments with her, he also has a dark and sordid corner in his neatly swept life, a place where nothing is labeled or put back in place. A corner unsupervised by Rekha.

Yet it is the safety of Rekha's banal certainties that Shiv longs for now. He couldn't tell her what happened today. He barely understands it himself, and besides, Meena was in the same room. Every word he said would have been like exposing himself to her, making himself vulnerable to her quick judgment.

For the moment, Shiv has to comfort himself with what Rekha might have said if he had confided in her: Take stock of the situation first. Don't commit yourself one way or the other. If you can't make a decision, go to bed and will yourself to sleep. And in the morning, be ruthless with yourself.

But Shiv knows there is no question of sleep. And he feels a little resentful, as if Rekha has actually said those words to him.

Mine is not a nine-to-five job like yours, he thinks. It may be late into the night but my day is not yet over.

The booklet is on Shiv's desk—the course booklet with the offending lesson. This is one lesson he does not need to reread to refresh his memory about what he wrote. It is, ironically, one of the few lessons he has written in his teaching career that was informed by genuine interest and historical curiosity.

Shiv tells himself he should leave the booklet alone and concentrate on the new one he has to write, the lesson on the end of the Vijayanagar empire. He pulls out the sheaf of notes he has on Vijayanagar. He forces himself to begin somewhere, anywhere. He writes on a blank sheet: Vijayanagar (or the City of Victory) was a medieval wonder-city, the capital of the wealthy Vijayanagar empire. The city was designed to be a showpiece of Hindu might. But its glory came to an end in 1565, when the city was sacked and left in ruins.

Shiv reads what he has written several times, searching for a clue to the next sentence. Then he puts his pen down. He wanders a little northward on the map; a little backward in time.

Three hundred kilometers north of Vijayanagar, almost three hundred years before the City of Victory rose and fell, there was another episode of glory and destruction. The terror and bloodshed in the two settings overlap; human suffering does not change all that much with time and circumstance. But glory—its meaning, its source—could not have been more different than it was for the treasurer of the Vijayanagar kingdom, and the treasurer of the twelfth-century city of Kalyana.

The treasurer of Kalyana was a man called Basava. This man was no ordinary finance minister. He had too much pas-

GITHA HARIHARAN

sion and charisma, too much vision, to remain a mere government official. Basava was plagued by questions; he needed to
examine and think through and criticize everything that was
traditional, *sanctioned,* as much as he needed to breathe. Basava
gathered around him a unique congregation of mystics and
social revolutionaries. Together they attempted a creative,
courageous experiment: a community that sought to exclude
no one—not women, not the lowest, most "polluting" castes.
Poets, potters, reformers, washermen, philosophers, prostitutes,
learned brahmins, housewives, tanners, ferrymen—all were
part of the brief burst of Kalyana's glory. All were equal in that
they were veerashaivas; warriors of Siva.

These warriors worked. They made pots and mirrors and
fishing nets and leather sandals. They ferried customers across
the river. They saw their work as part of their payment for a pas-
sage to Kailasa, where Siva lives. And the warriors made poetry,
poetry that chased prose; that searched passionately for the
many faces of truth. This poetry, which was also their scripture,
was called vachana: what was said. And it was said in Kannada,
not in exclusive Sanskrit. The vachanas were created and spoken and sung in a people's language, in words that were no
strangers to poor homes or dirty streets.

Basava and many of his followers took on the caste system,
the iron net that held society so firmly in place, that reduced the
common man and woman to hopeless captives. Thousands of
these "ordinary" men and women took part in Basava's egalitarian dream. The dream spread and took hold of people who had
not been *people* before in Kalyana, people who had just been
their functions: the makers of mirrors, the skinners of dead animals, the bearers of children. The people became a movement;
the movement swelled and surged, a wave that threatened to

swallow social conventions and religious ritual, staple diet of tradition. The king, Bijjala, an old friend of Basava's, was under tremendous pressure from the pillars of society. Not surprisingly, the relationship between the king and his finance minister soured.

The wave peaked, the story goes, when a marriage was arranged between the children of two veerashaiva couples. The bride-to-be was brahmin. The bridegroom-to-be was the son of a cobbler. This marriage is more the stuff of legend and folklore than stern history. But so apt a symbol was it of the crisis Basava's Kalyana was heading toward, that every subsequent popular account took the event for granted. The marriage is the ineluctable climax of the story in popular memory. (There is, however, ample historical evidence that Kalyana was rocked by violence in King Bijjala's last days.)

The story is that the marriage was the catalyst; it generated a shock that charged all of Kalyana City. The traditionalists were already enraged by Basava's challenge to their monopoly of god and power and the afterlife. Now, terrorized by their fear that "even a pig and a goat and a dog" could become a devotee of Siva in an equal society, they condemned this marriage as the first body blow against all things known, familiar, normal. Against, in short, a society based on caste. Egalitarian ideas are bad enough, but a cobbler and a brahmin in the same bed? As well bomb Kalyana (and its vigorous trade, its prosperous temples and palace) out of existence!

King Bijjala was pressured into joining the condemnation of the marriage. He sentenced the fathers of the bride and bridegroom (and the young untouchable bridegroom) to a special death. Tied to horses, they were dragged through the streets of Kalyana; then what was left of them was beheaded.

But Basava's followers did not call themselves warriors of Siva for nothing. They, particularly the young and the militant, particularly those who had shed the stigma of their lower caste status to become followers of Basava, retaliated. Basava's call for nonviolence was not heard. His charisma was no longer enough to keep the moderates and the extremists among his followers together.

The city burned; now in the untouchable potters' colonies, now in the coffer-heavy temples. Basava left the city for Kudalasangama, the meeting point of rivers that had been his inspiration in his youth. The king was assassinated, allegedly by two of Basava's young followers. Not long after King Bijjala's death, Basava too died under mysterious circumstances. The popular legend is that there, where the waters of the two rivers meet, the great river took him into its all-embracing arms.

Though veerashaivism would live on, its great moment of pushing for social change was over. What began as a critique of the status quo would be absorbed, bit by bit, into the sponge-like body of tradition and convention. But Basava and his companions left a legacy: a vision consisting of vigorous, modern thought; poetry of tremendous beauty and depth; images that couple the radical and the mystical. Most of all, Basava's passionate questions would remain relevant more than eight hundred years later.

In his deceptively quiet Delhi garden in the year 2000, Shiv considers Basava's legacy—a legacy he is now heir to in a sudden, unexpected way. Basava's dream broke up a long time ago, it no longer stands. But it was there. It lived. His movement for equality, for democracy, must be remembered, but so must its destruction; one without the other perverts memory. How is Shiv to explain Basava—his ideas, his times—to some bunch of hate-crazy goons? Or to Meena with her Said and Asterix, or even to Rekha with her sound instinct for the safe position?

Meena has not yet switched off the light in her room; she is probably waiting for Shiv to "chalk out" a plan. He will have to sneak upstairs to bed without her hearing him. And he has to think up a few answers for the Head and Dean tomorrow, anticipate their questions. Shiv sighs as he makes his way upstairs to his solitary bed.

One man in him wants to hit out, dazzle the Head and Dean into submission with Basava's courage and passion. *Certain gods always stand watch at the doors of people. Some will not go if you ask them to go. Worse than dogs, some others. What can they give, these gods, who live off the charity of people, O lord of the meeting rivers?*

But even as he recalls Basava's brave words, the other man in Shiv, the In-Charge of B.A. History, Rekha's predictable husband, strikes back in fear. He is an academic, he argues, not some rabble-rousing activist. He is a professor after all, not a two-inch newspaper column hero. Basava's man is ready with his rejoinder: Why pretend you are a professor if you can't stand up to someone telling you what to think? How to think? Shiv hears the apparently gentle tone, determined to be patient and reasonable, as persuasive as his own father used to be: Shiv, do you imagine an ordinary man cannot be a hero?

Shiv pulls the sheet over his head, shuts his eyes tight. He can't remember when last he felt so alone. Already he is looking back with nostalgia at life before the phone call: his editing Amita's module this morning, the secret, tentative pleasure of his lazy afternoon before the TV with Meena. All this is now what went before; a thing other than his actual life. Though he didn't know he was dreaming, the dream is coming to an end. When he wakes up tomorrow, he will wake, whether he is ready or not, to real life.

FIVE

SEPTEMBER 7

*I*n the morning, before the mirror. A soldier putting on armor to face the world with its Deans and Heads, and its wild and weedy protectors of history. Its Meenas, waiting for Shiv to turn into the club-wielding, foolhardy imitation of a mythical hero.

The reflection in the mirror is no hero, however. Nor is it a young man preening in well-fitting armor. It is fifty-two years old, an unlikely age for the birth of a hero. And the rest of the picture: medium height, soft-voiced, a stingy salt-and-pepper mustache, a gently swelling herbivorous paunch. Shiv hesitates as he pulls on his trousers—should he button and belt them above the bulge or below? He is not sure why he considers this choice afresh every morning. He always chooses to pull up his trousers anyway, hoist them well over his stomach, above the point where his waistline used to be. Hips seem unreliable. Trousers can fall.

· · ·

The Dean's office is a cool, soothing cave. Thick dark curtains, the dirt on them blending chameleon-like into the deep brown, shut out the university grounds. The Dean's room declares that he is a cultured man. The table, the chairs, the cupboards and bookshelves bear the required university branding in white paint. KGU-SS-32-1, says the painted corner of the Dean's table, a head of wooden livestock or a prisoner. All counted and accounted for. The Dean's furniture may be, in university offi-cialese, "as per regulations," but his room is different. The un-derstated earth colors of the ethnic prints on the wall, the dhurrie on the floor, the pen and staple and clip holders, the wooden vase with a dried-flower arrangement—all these signal that though he is a rising star in the university's Administration, he is not really one of them.

The Dean and the Head have been talking over cups of tea. There is a cup for Shiv, the skin on the liquid's surface announcing how long it has sat there waiting for its victim. The tea also tells him which chair to take; the Dean and the Head have decided where the defendant's dock is to be located. The Head sits on the chair beside Shiv's, across from the Dean; the Head seems to shrink away from Shiv, shift his chair a fraction to the right as if he might need a little more room. The Head's eyes take in Shiv's appearance in a quick, devious glance, then look away. The Dean, unsmiling but unfailingly courteous, says, "Come, Professor Murthy. Please take a chair. Tea?"

Shiv picks up the cup obediently and the Dean continues.

"I am sorry we had to ask you here while you are on leave. In fact, I am sorry we have to meet about this matter at all. But Professor Sharma must have told you the situation is getting serious."

The Head nods before Shiv can react. He seems mesmerized by the Dean's eloquence.

"Suppose we begin with what you have to say about this lesson. I have read it now, but I want to be absolutely sure that I present your version faithfully to the school board—and if it becomes necessary, to the University Governing Council."

Shiv takes a sip of the cold tea, which tastes as foul as it looks. Then he makes his reply exclusively to the Dean, ignoring the still nodding Head.

"The lesson is part of the module for the medieval Indian history paper, which carries three credits. Since the medieval period is my area, I preferred not to commission an outside expert to write the module. Though Basava is so many things, so many people rolled into one—poet and mystic, finance minister and political activist, man of the people and man of god— the lesson itself is quite straightforward. It traces the life of Basava. The growth of his radical ideas and his struggle against caste divisions and the temple establishment, the tensions that grew between the court and the brahmins and the merchants on the one hand, and on the other, the low-caste artisans and the untouchables who made up a large part of Basava's veerashaiva movement. The lesson ends with the crisis these tensions led to, and the dispersal of Basava's followers; and his own departure from Kalyana and his death shortly after."

The Dean listens to Shiv with interest, or perhaps a habitual simulation of it. But the Head (who is no longer nodding his head) is getting impatient.

"Yes, we've read the lesson, Dr. Murthy. The problem is not the text itself but the implications. What can be read between the lines. I have gone through the lesson carefully and I have made a list of the phrases and sentences that lend themselves to misinterpretation. I am afraid these lapses are what we will now have to explain."

He looks at Shiv severely; Shiv cannot believe he has thought of the Head as a diffident man all these years. As pompous but timid, perhaps pompous because he is timid. The man, having said goodbye to timidity, continues his harangue.

"One: Backward looking. Two: Contradictory accounts of Basava's life, conflicting narratives. Three: Birth legends fabricated. Four: Called a bigoted revolutionary by temple priests. Also called a dangerous man, a threat to structure, stability and religion. Five: The comfort of faith was not enough for Basava. Six: There were rumors that Basava used money from the royal treasury to look after his followers. Seven: The lines of social division in the great city of Kalyana were sharply drawn. Caste was a dominating factor. Eight: There was tension between the brahmanical religious orthodoxy and the popular religious reformers and saint-poets. Nine: Basava met and could have been influenced by the "mad men from Persia," the dancing, drinking Sufis. Ten: Bijjala, the king of Kalyana, was pressured by brahmin leaders to commit atrocities on low-caste devotees. Basava told the king a series of tales in which devotees, especially untouchable devotees, were shown to be superior to brahmins."

The Head stops to take a breath. The Dean, who has been listening with face bent over his tabletop, looks up.

"But all this *is* part of history, drawn from a variety of sources," Shiv says. "Part of the challenge of getting to know Basava's life and times is reconstructing it out of literary texts, legends, inscriptions and other records. The bibliography for the lesson includes all the major sources that have been used for quite some time now by medieval historians."

"Well," says the Dean. "We understand, Professor Murthy, and we are all agreed that this is most unfortunate. Professor Sharma, can we go through the demands of this Itihas Suraksha Manch?"

The Head probably has another sheet of what he likes to call ambiguous statements, as if the word *ambiguous* contains magic that automatically turns fact to falsehood. With an effort he tears himself away from the remainder of his list, and pulls out another sheet.

"The Manch has three demands. The first is an apology for hurting their sentiments. They want separate apologies from Dr. Murthy and from the Department, by extension the University. Second, the lesson should be retracted and the material recalled from all students registered in the course, and from study centers and libraries. Third, the rewritten lesson should be submitted to the Manch before it is sent to our printing unit."

The Dean frowns. "We can't submit material to them for approval. That's outrageous and they know it. My hunch is that they are testing the waters to see how far they can go."

The Head's silence seems to indicate agreement, but Shiv is no longer sure of this man. In times where paranoia lives in the same air everyone must breathe, it is difficult to say who is "going soft" and who is simply a man who dislikes trouble. And the Head is sixty-one, just a year short of retirement. If he is anxious to get an extension as a consultant, he will want his last year as Head unsullied by controversy.

"I will not apologize," Shiv suddenly says. "I do not say anything about the other two demands, partly because they do not involve just me."

The Head looks at Shiv as if he is a pesky fly that needs swatting. Shiv can feel his resolve hardening. Maybe he will regret it later, but he is damned if he will let the Head think he can be brought into line so easily. Shiv clears his throat and says again, clearly, "The lesson does not distort history by any stretch of the imagination. And I will not apologize or explain myself to a group outside the university, a group of people we do not recognize as historians."

The Head snaps at Shiv, "I didn't know you hankered to be a hero, Dr. Murthy. We are middle-aged professors, not stunt-men." The Head would never have guessed that Shiv had exactly this thought just the night before. Now more than ever the Head prefers the world in clear black and white. But he also sees the Dean's eyebrows rise; the Head swiftly changes tracks.

"We are here," he says, "to standardize knowledge. This does not contradict our commitment to historical authenticity." Then the Head gets off the soapbox and gets to the point. "And besides, who has this lesson been written for? The readers are only B.A. students."

He does not say "only correspondence students" though the thought must cross his mind.

He says instead, "As for the historical facts, what are the facts pertinent to the lesson? One: Kalyana *was* a glorious Hindu kingdom, a little peak, if you like, of the Hindu past and heritage. Two: Basava taught people the importance of uplifting the untouchables, but he was the founder of a religion, not some radical screaming for revolution. Why not stick to these facts? Our students need to know dates, the achievements of great saints and kings. Why get into debates and controversies—however fascinating, however historically permissible—if the students don't need these or appreciate them? Our university simply cannot afford self-indulgence. When we have students from across India and from so many different back-grounds, we have to guard against irresponsible controversies."

"But Dr. Sharma," Shiv says, nettled by this talk of self-indulgence, "We can hardly pretend that the chaos in Kalyana was not the result of a movement for social change. We can hardly pretend there was no fundamental division between the interests of the ruling brahmins and the growing number of low-caste veerashaiva devotees. Or that Basava was not a man of his times, shaped by its limitations and moved by the need to overcome its oppressors. I realize you are concerned about dam-age control, and I share this concern, but I don't believe the problem is historical method."

The Dean does not disagree with either of them. All his face says is that he would not have chosen the Head's way of putting it, or Shiv's for that matter. Now he says to them like a reluctant umpire, "Professor Murthy has told us in no uncertain terms that he is against a personal apology. I don't think we can be hasty about this. Professor Murthy, though time is of the essence if we are to scotch this effectively, I don't want you to feel pressurized. Why don't you think it over for a few days?"

As Shiv stands up, the Dean too rises. They shake hands formally as if Shiv is setting out on a long journey. Shiv leaves the room before the Head and walks back to his car, frustrated and dissatisfied. Amita is right, thinks Shiv. There is such a thing as post-meeting blues—because most meetings never get beyond monologues to discussion. Yet what would they have discussed at the Dean's office? How to write history? Or, as Meena and her friends would have it, how to fight the obscurantists?

. . .

Once in the car, Shiv decides he will not go home. Instead he drives to the next parking lot, adjacent to the building housing the Department. Though he did not plan to go there today, now it seems right that he should go to his room, sit in his chair, check his mail, assert territorial rights.

The first person he sees while fumbling with the lock on his door is the Head's secretary. Mrs. Khan smiles at him, sunny and warm as ever. "Checking your mail, Dr. Murthy?" she asks.

But though they greet each other and exchange pleasantries for the usual three minutes, no more, no less, Shiv senses that they are playing at normalcy. Or is this a figment of his imagination, these infinitesimal islands of wariness that have floated to the surface of her eyes and his, two different islands with the same tainted flora?

Whether it is fact or fiction, Shiv watches her receding back with some relief. There is an invisible little badge, a mark, something akin to shame that draws two victims together. Yet each finds the mirror image of the stain repulsive in the other.

Shiv shuts the door, sits down at his desk and looks around him. At the familiar bookshelves with their weight of colorful spines, the shelves sagging in the middle with their decade-long burden. The glass-fronted cupboard, the filing cabinet. KGU-DOH-SS29, KGU-DOH-SS30. The walls, painted a blue that made him seasick till it faded with the assistance of time, dust and dirt. High up on the wall before him, close to the ceiling, the two damp patches that make a large reclining figure of eight. So persistent are these peeling patches that they have been in this room as long as Shiv. He has, over the years, seen different pictures in them, as if the patches make up a private version of the Rorschach test. Their shape has helped him imagine great big breasts; lungs; a pair of wings.

Shiv's eyes turn to the adjacent wall with two windows. He can hear cooing at the windowsill that the pigeons share with his cooler. He has been at war with these pigeons forever. But they continue to exercise tenancy rights, nesting by the cooler and using its top as a runway to take off into the skies.

A wistful sigh escapes Shiv's lips. This is where he belongs. This is where he wants to be. The thought comes in a flash of surprised recognition. This must be how a man feels when he has leapt out of an open window. The last image he sees before his picture-making machine hits the pavement and breaks, is a message flashed in telegraphic language: I know I complained, but I didn't mean it, or not as much as I thought I did; I belong in that room up there after all.

Shiv hears a knock on the door and before he can react, Amita Sen opens the door; he can see Menon just behind her. Mrs. Khan has been quick to spread the word.

"Shiv," says Amita, her voice plaintive as if she is crying for help. "How are you—I am so glad to see you."

"How did the meeting go? What are we going to do?" asks Menon. The two of them come in, sit down. Amita immediately pulls a packet of cigarettes and a lighter out of her kurta pocket.

Sympathy, curiosity, excitement. Amita's chronic boredom has vanished. Menon, enigmatic Menon who can spend a whole meeting staring at the ceiling in a trance, is actually agitated. Shiv stops himself: why is he dissecting their sympathy to make sure it is unadulterated? These are his colleagues, his friends. If he shrinks from them, from their probing questions and solemn condoling looks, who is left? Where is he to find sustenance for an encounter he is unprepared for?

Shiv tells them briefly what was said. In the recounting, he sees once again how meager the contents of the meeting were. If he is to learn generosity, a different kind of generosity that will allow him to share his troubles with friends, make himself vulnerable, he will have to do better than this. He will have to consult Amita and Menon on his plan of action.

Plan of action. The phrase brings to mind, with sharp clarity, a smooth face framed by thick long waves. Shiv's tongue moves to the floor of his mouth. It searches for something tart and juicy, like the tamarind pods he used to bite into as a child. The taste brings to mind a bare brown leg. A cast. Meena. Shiv sneaks a look at Amita who is blowing perfect circles of smoke into the air between them. For an instant memory summons up another taste, the taste of Amita's nicotine-laced tongue. Then he feels a twinge of disloyalty, though he is not sure whom he feels disloyal to.

"I'll be in touch with the two of you," he says, picking up his keys. Menon, like the Dean, shakes Shiv's hand; then, unlike the Dean, he pats Shiv's shoulder.

There is an awkwardness to their goodbyes, as if Menon and Amita are visiting him on Death Row. A part of Shiv wants to laugh. It's just some lunatic fringe flexing their muscles in the wrong arena. Why is everyone taking it so seriously, acting as if battle is imminent? Are they not empowering the loonies by paying attention to them? After all, Shiv and his friends have laughed at so many imaginative samples of chauvinism in the recent past: The United States was originally a nation of Hindus. Jesus preached his Sermon on the Mount in Kashmir. St. Paul's Cathedral was actually a temple built by Sant Pal. Not so long ago, Amita would ask Arya with a wicked grin, "Why do you have a calculator, Dr. Arya? I thought you could do it all in your head with Vedic math?"

It is when Shiv is driving back home that he remembers Arya. It is only now that he notices that neither Menon nor Amita mentioned him; nor did the Head for that matter; or, obviously, Mrs. Khan. Arya seems to have dissolved into thin air. Dissolved into a thousand molecules hanging patiently, cunningly, in the air that surrounds them.

At home, Meena, hobbling on her crutches, opens the door for Shiv.

"Where's Kamla?" he asks her. "Or Babli?"

But Meena is too excited to notice his concern that she has been left alone. "They're around somewhere—I don't know. But look at what you've got. Both delivered by hand. Babli took them, so unfortunately I didn't see the messenger."

Shiv helps Meena to a chair, then takes the two envelopes from her. Both have been opened.

"I knew you wouldn't mind," says Meena, "I couldn't bear to wait till you came home. But read them. Read the longer one first."

The longer one is the first page of *Current,* and the article on the bottom end of the page has been marked heavily with a red felt-tip pen.

Who will teach the teacher?
Protests against Prof's Distortion of History
New Delhi, September 6: A senior professor of history at the Kasturba Gandhi Central University (KGU) in New Delhi has been charged with distorting facts and introducing an ideological bias into a lesson in the University's medieval Indian history course.

The Itihas Suraksha Manch, an independent social and cultural organization, issued a statement on Wednesday in the capital calling for "an end to tampering with our precious and glorious Indian history." The statement, signed by one of the organization leaders, Mr. Anant Tripathi, said, "We will not allow our history to be polluted like this. Fifty years after independence, we cannot have Indian historians brainwashed by foreign theories and methods depriving us of our pride in Hindu temples and priests. How are these historians different from the Muslims who invaded our land? Every school child knows the story of the Mohammeds, from Ghazni to Ghori. Muslim invaders have always tried to destroy Hindu pride and civilization. In the same way, these modern invaders pretending to be historians are attacking our system of traditions and our way of life that have stood the test of time. But this time we will not allow ourselves to be conquered and subjected. We will make sure our history remains a way to show the world examples of our great Hindu past."

The Manch also quoted several historians, including retired Professor Shri A. A. Atre, to support their claim that "Basava was not against brahmins as such." All he wanted, like any saint, was that everyone should live in order and harmony. The venerable professor told reporters in Pune, "To say that the saint Basava may have died 'in broken, disillusioned exile' is as much a mischievous distortion of history as to say that he may have learnt anything from the Muslim sufis of Persia. Sad to say, there seem to be scholars with vested interests who think the treasures of our past can be taken away from us."

The KGU historian, Professor Shiv Murthy, has gone on leave since the protests began. He refused to confirm whether the University had asked him to go on leave or whether he will resign from the Department. He also claimed to be unaware of the furor caused by his text. On the question of the historian's responsibility to society, his response was a terse "No comment." Professor A. A. Atre has condemned this reaction as "sheer arrogance."

"It's completely insane, isn't it? This Atre must be some senile stooge they have pulled out of hibernation," says Meena, peering into Shiv's face for a suitably enraged reaction. The muscles on his face refuse to oblige. He can feel his left eye twitch.

"Read the other one," Meena urges him. "It's the first of the hate mail."

Shiv reads obediently. The letter, unstamped, is typed on a yellow postcard. (It's been so long since he saw one of these postcards that he has a bizarre sense of having gone back in time.) The sender's name is missing.

Dear Respected Murthyji, (it begins.)

It is a tragedy that an educated person like you should indulge in ignorant and unpatriotic acts. This is the least I can say after giving you benefit of the doubt about your sincerity as a teacher.

If you want to rewrite Indian history with our Hindu saints as cowards and failures in exile, why not go to Pakistan and do it? They will welcome you and give you all attention and praise you are desperate for.

After seeing your disrespect for our glorious temples and their priests, and your attempt to reduce our saints to mere men, I can only conclude that you are trying to undermine Hinduism. What are you trying to say? That the Muslims are great? In which case I have three questions to ask you, Respected Professorji. Do you have a wife and daughter? How would you feel if they became a Muslim's playthings? Will you still write the same history?

Shiv puts both these gems back in the brown envelopes they came in. He notices the envelopes have his name and residential address neatly typed on them. Yellow journalism and anonymous poison mail, all in one day. And is this just the beginning? Is there worse to come? He hates the thought of some stranger, some nameless hoodlum warped by heartburn, in possession of his address. Suddenly his address holds in its three innocuous lines all the intimate details of his life to date. There is a sour taste in his mouth; it occurs to him that he has not eaten or drunk anything since that sip of cold tea in the Dean's office. He feels a mad desire for a tall cold glass of juice; something orangey, something that will cleanse his tongue. Then sleep, lots of it.

But first he has to report, for the second time today, on the meeting in the Dean's office. Meena, too young to hold back her news, has welcomed him home with the newspaper clipping and the postcard. But it is what the Dean is prepared to do, and what the university decides, that matter most. Shiv reminds himself of this lest he begin to believe it is him versus all the out-of-work fundamentalists and crazies in the world.

Meena hears him out, but she has already made up her mind about how the meeting went. "Your Head is typical," she says to Shiv. "These liberal fence-sitters! One whiff of danger and they fall off the fence, over to the wrong side."

But with just two little previews of what is possibly to come, the anger Shiv felt earlier this morning has lost its edge. Though the Head can be a tiresome pompous ass, Shiv thinks, he can't be condemned so easily. But what can Shiv say to defend the Head at the moment? And what is the point playing at fairness and objectivity when all the world knows only crude divisions, black and white, friend and enemy?

"I've called Amar," Meena tells Shiv. "You remember Amar, he came to see me the other day. He is an activist and a committed member of several citizens' groups. We have discussed the *Current* article and he thinks a citizens' forum should take it up. I am supposed to ring him up and confirm when we can have a meeting here."

But it's another phone call Shiv is concerned about. The phone in the living room is still not working, and Shiv can no longer wait to call Rekha. It's already five in the evening. Luckily, Meena has been too excited and busy to wash in the morning. Now, as she pulls on her bathtime plastic to cover the cast, Shiv quickly calculates the time difference between Delhi and Seattle. The minute Meena hobbles into the bathroom, he picks up the phone, dials.

The sound of Rekha's voice—calm and poised in spite of being woken up—is infinitely reassuring. "It's a beautiful morning here," she says. "Tara is taking the day off to show me the Space Needle."

"But she's just got this job, can she take time off already?" he asks, strangely reluctant to let go of the momentary illusion of normalcy. Rekha sounds so unsuspecting, so innocent somehow. How is he to shatter that even if it means sharing the worry with her? And where is he to begin, how is he to explain that his life may change—and hers—all for a history lesson?

"Rekha, I told you Sumati's daughter is here, didn't I? Kamla has been very helpful, but she got sick and I've taken leave for a bit—just to help out."

"You're going to help Kamla?" Rekha laughs. "Since when did you start helping with housework?"

This is no way to get to the matter. Meena will be out of the bathroom soon. Shiv's voice changes as he tries to keep it matter-of-fact and firmly under control. "Rekha, there's a problem here."

But his voice has already alerted Rekha. "It's not Meena or Kamla, something has happened at the university. Hasn't it, Shiv?"

"Yes," he says, relieved, the words now tumbling out of him. "It's one of my medieval history units—a lesson I wrote on Basava. I've read some of his poems to you, do you remember?

But there's some mad group called the Itihas Suraksha Manch of all things, and they've got hold of the lesson and they claim it has hurt their feelings . . ."

Rekha waits in puzzled silence.

"They want me to apologize and the university to withdraw the lesson." Shiv pauses. Meena is out of the bathroom; her crutches are tapping their way to her bed. He manages an awkward laugh. "I actually got hate mail today, can you believe it?"

Rekha does not lag behind Meena for a swift response. "What nonsense," she says scornfully. "Sounds like rubbish to me. Throw out the hate mail and complain to university security. I think you're worrying too much as usual."

"Maybe I am," says Shiv hesitantly, willing himself to believe her. He sees that Meena has got into bed, freshly washed, wide-awake. "But I had to meet the Head and the Dean today."

Rekha has met the Head and refuses to take him seriously. How can she when the poor fellow is so solemn and deliberate that it takes him all of five minutes to say hello? "What does that Dean of yours say?" she asks.

"Nothing much, it was mostly the Head who held forth. You know how he is. But I've told the Dean I won't apologize, and now it's up to the university—we'll have to wait and see, they don't want a controversy."

"Of course," says Rekha a little dryly. "I don't suppose anyone does."

Shiv suspects Rekha has not fully understood what is going on, but then nor has he. And he has not explained the kind of Arya-tainted atmosphere in the university. But still, for the moment, he stops worrying about the Head and the Dean and the unknown Manch. All day Shiv has been buffeted about, vacillating between disbelief and anger, amusement and fear. Now he sits alone in the dark garden, a lit mosquito coil at his feet, a glass of whisky in his hand. Though he has not begun on her list of things to do, Rekha's garden is an orderly refuge. In its peaceful quiet, he can approach, however tentatively, the real issue at hand: how he, as a historian, sees Basava; and how he, as a man, is to survive this interpretation.

Things standing shall fall, but the moving shall ever stay. Every word of Basava's was a challenge, both to himself and to those around him. The heroic mode. In a building, in a city, in a man. In men, growing into empire. Who is a hero? A leader? What makes some of us speak out, draw others to listen?

Where is the country that breeds heroes? Does it have a place on a map?

As if he has heard his questions, Shiv's father, meticulous answerer of difficult questions, wanders into his mind. Shiv knew his father for only the first thirteen years of his life. He has had to stretch memory, fill in blank spaces and obliterate stubborn question marks, to fashion his father's life into a viable narrative.

There are some things his father used to say to Shiv—often, he imagines, from the clarity with which he recalls them still. It is these words Shiv now draws on to reconstruct his father's private mythology. Freedom. Values. The common good. "You must mine the truth," his father would say. "If you settle for safety, if you choose to go along with whatever makes your life comfortable, truth will escape you completely. Shiva: there is a kind of person who lives like this. He is called an opportunist. Repeat the word after me so you remember it. Op-por-tun-ist."

Memory. Its relationship with history. How much memory should a historian bear on his back? In spite of his exhortations to courage, his father's life—incomplete, cut off without a legible end—is a tail-less example of a man with too much memory. He was delighted to find that Shiv had inherited his good memory. "You must study history," he told Shiv. "You must know the past with all its riches and terrors, draw on the lessons of both in equal measure."

But how do you seize hold of the past and make it yours? Who owns the past?

SIX

SEPTEMBER 8–17

*M*orning, a clear day. The gentle blue sky is the picture of innocence. The curtain by Meena's bed has been pushed aside to let the day in. Meena's bed is a friendly, rumpled nest of sheets and pillows. Babli is in this nest, her face a mask of delight. Meena has given her a set of felt-tip markers all the colors of the rainbow, and she has hitched up her skirt to one side so that her entire cast is Babli's canvas.

Babli is hard at work. Her tongue sticks out of her mouth, stiff with concentration. She is growing an instant garden, a garden in the shape of a leg. A made-up garden, no relative of the one Rekha has commissioned in their backyard. Babli's garden boasts brilliant blue flowers and extravagant orange leaves. Yellow-winged butterflies hang in the air, suspended in mid-flight. Their wings are tipped with brown oval eyes. A blazing crimson sunflower sits comfortably on Meena's broken knee. Its petals are thick and succulent, holders of healing magic. Meena is in charge of the greening of this burgeoning garden. The color pen in her hand traces green vines. She connects Babli's floating creations with a twisting, creeping network of veins, linking them all on the undulating landscape of her thigh and knee.

They see Shiv, these smooth-faced guardians of paradise, but do not see that he is only a spectator at their innocent feast of colors. "Here, choose a color," Meena invites him. She picks up a dark-brown marker from the bed and waves it in his direction. He takes it from her hand.

The thigh and knee are now crowded, all the new tenants held in place by Meena's green vine. Babli has moved down to the foreleg. She is drawing a full-blown flower, every petal an elongated swollen finger.

Shiv perches on the edge of the bed at Meena's feet. "Babli's got butterflies but no bees," says Meena with a grin. "Come on, we have a job for you. We need a bee for Babli's fat flower." Babli giggles and puts the last stroke on her flower with a flourish.

Shiv pulls off the lid of his color pen. The felt tip smells of nail varnish, a mildly intoxicating smell. He bends over Meena's leg and identifies the small white patch where he will import his bee into their paradise. What he manages to draw is a nameless wormlike creature, hanging like a stiff umbrella over Babli's flower. Babli then shows him how to complete it. Yellow stripes, fuzz, wings, stick-legs, waving antennae.

His brief hour of reprieve, the comforting calm before the storm, spent in the secret garden of wise children. Then it all begins again. The world outside the small room stirs, raises its hood. The phone rings.

. . .

It is Menon from the Department.

"Shiv? Have you heard what has happened?"

"No, but it's too soon for anything to happen, Menon. For once I'm grateful the university doesn't move fast."

"But it has, Shiv. Didn't Amita call you? I spoke to her and she was very upset."

"Tell me, then we can all be upset together." (Shiv is still in the room with bees, flowers, one-legged girls. This is only his shadow holding on to a prosaic telephone.)

A rueful chuckle from Menon, who then says, "It's not funny, I'm afraid. Mrs. Khan told me she saw an official letter about you from the VC to the Head. The booklet containing your module is being sent for review to some so-called expert committee, all very hush-hush, no one even knows the names of these experts. And the Head seems to have decided that till this happens, students should be asked to return their copies of the material."

"But how can he do this on his own? The Dean said to wait for a few days and I don't see how anything can be done without consulting me. I am in charge of B.A. History, after all."

"Shiv, that's the worst of it. Apparently the Head and the Dean have been advised by higher-ups—not our university bigwigs but the real ones—that your resignation may be the only way to satisfy the Manch."

"Till the next time they strike?"

"Yes," agrees Menon gloomily. "It's like waking up in a world full of Aryas. Don't do anything hasty, Shiv. Will you come to the Department tomorrow?"

"Probably. And Menon? Thanks." It has suddenly dawned

on Shiv how hateful it must have been for Menon, who never says a word more than he has to, to gossip with Mrs. Khan, make telephone calls, play tale-carrier.

An hour later, he has the letter. It is exactly as Menon said.

"They can't make you resign!" exclaims Meena, the letter on her lap. That wretched piece of paper on her vividly painted leg: the proximity of the two worlds hurts Shiv.

"No, they can't," he tells her. "That's why I am merely being asked to 'cooperate,' as the Head puts it. To 'bring the unfortunate controversy to an end.'"

"But calling back the lesson? Can they do that?"

"We've done it before a couple of times, but it's always been a faculty decision. Never because of mob censorship." Shiv frowns. "I suppose I could get legal advice." He pulls at his mustache doubtfully. "But I don't know if that will be of any use, the copyright of the module is with the university."

Shiv imagines his lesson sent to the corner in disgrace. Booklet lies upon booklet in the printing unit storeroom, waiting to be pulped. There is a warning sign that quarantines it from the other booklets, a sign like the ones on those ominously shaped vehicles carrying dangerous chemicals. Caution! Highly Inflammable Medieval History. Only known antidotes: 500 mg of blissful ignorance or 250 mg of unadulterated lies.

Shiv's booklets have been banished, along with the real—and troublesome—Basava. Only a sanitized Basava is allowed to remain, a "saint-singer," a singer with a saintly face. This toothless man is safe enough to be hung on walls, a bland calendar memory. He is incapable of demanding shrewdly, threateningly, like the real Basava Shiv has glimpsed through the glass pane of history and poetry: *If you risk your hand with a cobra in a pitcher, will it let you pass?*

The irony of it takes Shiv's breath away: to sanctify Basava and gloss over caste, all in one breath! But it's not as if the Manch is the first to distort Basava's life and memory. The Basava Shiv wrote about, tried to introduce his students to, was a man who elicited extreme reactions, both during his times and much later. He was, all too often, either deified, or demonized. For the purveyors of magic (and their subsect of zealots) Basava's life unfolds in a haze of legend. It was Lord Siva who sent him down to earth. The usual birth legends have been fabricated; the usual early-precociousness lore and self-sufficiency tales proliferate. Demigods are easier to co-opt into the pantheon of gods once they die. (Demigods do not end up as political prisoners; they do not end their lives in broken, disillusioned exile.) For the detractors and demonizers, Basava was nothing more (and nothing less villainous) than a bigoted revolutionary. A man obsessed with upsetting tradition. A dangerous man, a threat to structure, stability, religion. To the way things have always been, so the way things should always be.

Wading through the numerous contradictory accounts of Basava's life means parting several meeting rivers. Separating history and myth, pulling apart history and legend. Deciding which chunks of history will keep the myth earthbound; which slivers of myth will cast light, and insight, on dull historical fragments. The two have to be torn apart, their limbs disentangled, to see who is who; then coaxed into embrace again to understand the composite reality. Approaching the whole, the heterogeneous truth that demands the coupling of conflicting narratives, requires the participation of more than one body.

But for the moment Shiv has no idea how to make the leap from his Basava lesson, or his own confused thoughts on reconstruction, to the eager, competent bodies congregating in Meena's room.

Shiv recognizes Amar, the tall young man who seems to be their undisputed leader, as the friend Meena described as a "committed activist." Everything about Amar is on a big scale. All his features are drawn with bold, well-defined strokes. From a distance, he looks like one of those monolithic idols carved out of a single, powerful rock.

Amar and his friends sit around Meena's bed, drawing up lists of "progressive" historians, academics, journalists, MPs. The room is already beginning to look like a campaign office: headquarters. The phone is passed around, since all of them seem to receive as many calls as they make.

"Getting the front together," Amar kindly explains to Shiv. Shiv would like to help his unsolicited helpers, say something that will make their support worth their while. He would also like to assure them that there is no case; that there is nothing controversial about the lesson. Instead he mumbles something about tea for everyone and escapes to the kitchen, grateful that Kamla is not around.

"What we need is a hard-hitting press conference," Amar says to Shiv when he returns bearing tea. "We should move quickly so we beat them to it."

"Let me discuss it with my colleagues," Shiv says. "Let me think about it a little."

If only he, Shiv, could be Meena or Amar for a day, distill all complexities to the breadth and weight of one sentence: "The same people who can't hiccup without consulting caste rules don't want it talked about in textbooks." But instead, a cast like the one on Meena's leg is being wrapped around Shiv, a cast that immobilizes him completely. It is not as if he is just being asked to prove he is a historian. It's the other demands of proof—from two different corners of the ring—that freeze Shiv, slow his heart to a standstill. Proof on the one hand that he is patriotic, Hindu, Indian; proof on the other that he can say and do the right things, transform himself into a twenty-first century echo of the dissenting Basava.

University calls back medieval history

New Delhi, September 10: In a controversial move, the Kasturba Gandhi Central University (KGU) has asked its students to return a booklet of lessons on medieval Indian history. The booklet contains a lesson on the saint-singer Basavanna's social reform movement by KGU historian Prof. Shiv Murthy, who has been charged with distorting historical figures as well as the caste system by an organization called the Itihas Suraksha Manch.

The University authorities denied that asking their correspondence students to return the material amounted to meeting the demands of the Manch. A statement issued on Monday by the University claimed that "the use of the course material has only been temporarily suspended, pending review by an expert committee. The University stands by the academic credentials of all its faculty, including Prof. Shiv Murthy, who is a senior member of its History Department."

A deep-rooted conspiracy, say Manch leaders

New Delhi, September 11: The leader of the Itihas Suraksha Manch, Mr. Anant Tripathi, today described Prof. Shiv Murthy's lesson on Basavanna as "part of a deep-rooted conspiracy to defame Hindu saints in particular and Hindu history and culture in general."

He charged Prof. Murthy with deliberately picking up controversial strands of the Indian past like caste and targeting brahmins and temples in his version of history. "There have been attempts for quite some time by so-called secular people, all of whom are interested in obtaining foreign funding, to project Hinduism in an incorrect and defamatory manner."

He refused to comment when asked if non-historians could judge learning material produced by qualified scholars, or when asked if this was censorship of liberal voices in academia.

Call to revive Hindu courage

New Delhi, September 12: Following a statement yesterday by Mr. Anant Tripathi of the Itihas Suraksha Manch, the junior vice-president of the Manch gave a call to "revive Hindu courage."

"We have to shed the cowardice that has grown in us with Muslims, then Europeans storming Indian shores. Though Hindus were among the bravest of the ancient peoples, repeated outside conquests have made them cowards. Even Mahatma Gandhi said so. We want to make the Hindu strong and courageous again. A meek person cannot survive. I am not only talking about muscle power. We must return to our old militant spirit if the Hindu nation is to become great again. We must spread moral and spiritual strength in the younger generation by taking teachings of courage and valor to schools and colleges."

The modules and lessons that were the stuff of Shiv's normal life are now replaced by newspapers. He subscribes to five newspapers instead of his usual two; he feels compelled to read every inch of them, as if they will tell him exactly what to expect next. And *Current* continues to send him relevant little bits to remind him that they have not forgotten him. He would like to throw these sickeningly familiar red-marked "news items" in the garbage without reading them. But in fact he reads them so carefully that the newsprint leaves dirty smudges on his hands. Who else but *Current* can tell him, for instance, that the Children of Saints Society in Guntur, Andhra Pradesh, have an exclusive hotline to the past? With a confidence that would be the envy of any historian, their press release says: Our Basavanna was a great man sent to earth by Siva himself to do his work among men. There was no question of whether he would succeed or fail, so where is the question of his dying alone in exile? Anyone who refuses to see this must be punished.

"I suppose I should read the famous lesson," Meena says to Shiv, grinning mischievously. "I will, but will you give me a quick précis for now so I know what's making the children of saints froth at the mouth?"

Is there a single image, a simple one that will hold his knowledge of Basava? Shiv imagines a hospitable tree, the kind that attracts all sorts of vines and creepers. It is impossible to look at this tree, visualize it in all its wealth of detail, if the vines and creepers are cut out of the picture. But what happens when the parasites grow too thick and lush, when they rob the tree of all nourishment? The tree sickens; it dies a lingering death. The hagiographies—the creepers—are an inevitable part of any reconstruction, historical or literary, of Basava's life. But—and Shiv pulls himself back from his verdant fantasy to the waiting Meena—the Aryas and Atres and all their thought-shrinking police pretend the parasite is the tree. They use the creepers to prettify the picture; whitewash it; or even better, use them like brushes dipped in magic paint. It's safer that way.

"You want Basava nugget-size," says Shiv to Meena. "I don't know if that's possible. Let's stick to the problem instead—why it is difficult to remember a man like Basava." Shiv would like to match Meena's light tone, but his words sound pedantic even to himself. "Let me put it this way: take a man who asked uncomfortable questions, a man who challenged the caste-ridden ground you walk on. Luckily the man cannot come back and snap his fingers at you when you speak on his behalf. So turn him into a saint-poet, into someone floating in a heavenly limbo. Turn a leader into a minor god; the man into a saint.

That's the only way to make him safely untouchable. Then his ideas and politics need not be understood; they won't make your life uncomfortable. The lessons his life holds—what he saw then and what we see now in hindsight—no longer have to be recalled. Or put into practice."

Academics protest withdrawal of history lesson

New Delhi, September 13: The decision to withdraw a lesson on the medieval reformer Basavanna by KGU professor Shiv Murthy has sparked a round of sharp criticism in academic circles.

The lesson, part of the B.A. History program, has been used by the correspondence university's students for the last five years as part of a paper on medieval Indian history. The official statement is that the lesson has been temporarily withdrawn for review by an expert committee, and makes no mention of the protests the lesson has drawn from the Itihas Suraksha Manch. But academic circles are abuzz with speculation that "orders from above" may be the reason for the unprecedented university decision to review the lesson.

On Wednesday, a large number of academics, including eminent historians Amit Kumar Mookherjee, N. A. Parthasarathy and Amir Qureishi, deplored this action.

They said it was "clear this was a response to

the demands of the Manch. These demands actually add up to a plan to perpetrate a fictitious and homogenous 'golden Hindu history' that will legitimize their program of one language, one religion, one nation. We condemn the University's failure to take a firm stand against this kind of blatant intellectual censorship, which can only lead to further targeting of secular historians."

"I never thought my little lesson on Basava would grow to such epic proportions," Shiv says to Meena.

"Lesson? Who's worrying about a single lesson," she says.

He pulls a wry face but he too sees that the lesson has been submerged in the meeting rivers. So has Basava, one more time. Now the case—or the cause—has grown like a spider's web. Its sticky spittle has moved on to new threads.

Now it's no longer caste and temple, or even contesting narratives of an enigmatic historical figure. Now the stage is littered with Muslim invaders, Christian missionaries, sons of the soil, and foreigners. The stage has grown and grown till it is a battlefield big enough for the new patriots and their wild and warped nationalistic dreams.

Their dream sequences scorn the banal existence of well-known facts. Their imaginations work overtime concocting febrile memories: horsedrawn chariots thousands of years before their invention. Hymns packed with occult allusions to high-energy physics and calculations of the speed of light. All part of a hoary, unashamedly golden past. A past *past-er* than anybody else's, so how can it not be the cradle of all civilization?

. . .

Shiv's own battlefield has its moments of grandeur.

He hears the doorbell. A few minutes later, Kamla comes rushing upstairs. Her pale, flu-ravaged face is suddenly colored with animation. "TV people, Sahib," she announces in an excited whisper. "They have come to take your interview."

"I'll be there in a while," he tells her. "Will you give them something to drink?"

"Of course," she says, her voice filled with injured reproach. "Do you need to tell me something like that? And Sahib, your shirt, it's not—it hasn't been ironed properly. Let me take another one for you from the cupboard."

The camera downstairs has finally proved his worth to Kamla. If the TV people want him, he must be a truly desirable sahib, the kind you can work for head held high. Poor Babli, away at school, will be heartbroken when she hears what she has missed.

"My shirt's alright, Kamla. They said they'll be here for just five minutes." She purses her mouth disapprovingly as if to say, If you miss your big chance, don't say I didn't warn you.

Downstairs, the living room is transformed. The curtains are drawn; there is a spotlight on a chair, all the light in the room sucked into that one dusty white beam. The floor is criss-crossed with thick snaky wires and cables. Shiv steps over them carefully, dodges batteries, lights, camera and assistants.

A young woman gets up from the chair and shakes his hand. "Professor Murthy? I am Priya. I spoke to you on the phone about a short interview for our program." She hands over a card that Shiv puts in his pocket. He looks at her and the strangely lit room about him with hesitation.

"Where would you be comfortable? This is just an informal interview. How about this chair?" Shiv sits down obediently. One of the men clips a little beetle-like mike on his shirt.

"I will ask you two or three questions which will then be edited out. Please speak to me—I'll sit here—and not to the camera." She indicates where she will sit, outside the camera's field of vision.

For the next half-hour Shiv sits frozen on the chair while the cameraman fiddles with his lens and the girl discusses the shot with him. Shiv hears snatches of their conversation as the lightman and his assistant try an assortment of beams on his face. "No, leave that shadow, open the screen. Jasjit, check the background."

"Sir, can we move the chair a little, just in front of the bookshelf?"

The mike-man hurries forward to help Shiv hold on to the wire that leashes him to the man's machine. Now Shiv is a professor in front of his bookshelf. A man wearing his appropriate suit of armor. He smiles at the thought and the girl catches his eye. "It looks very good now," she assures him. "Jasjit, bring that gamla here." Jasjit, his feet caged in sneakers of an impressive size, sets down one of Rekha's plants next to Shiv's chair. A nice touch: now he is a man wearing his bookish armor, let loose in a leafy jungle.

All the lights are on. A cool stream of sweat rolls down the back of Shiv's neck. He pulls out his handkerchief and mops his face.

"We'll begin then, sir."

"Yes," says Shiv, having lost faith by now. But a man switches off the fan, all the lights in the world seek out Shiv's chair before the bookshelf, and the girl sits across from him, smiling reassuringly as she says, "Professor Murthy, welcome to *Newslight*. Could you introduce yourself in a few words?"

Having spent the last sweaty half-hour wondering how to compress the writing of history and Basava's life and ideas into five minutes, this beginning unsettles Shiv.

"Yes, well, I am a historian," he says. (His father lurks in the shadows by the curtains. Shiv sees him still and intent, his eyes never leaving his son's face.) "I teach history at the Kasturba Gandhi Central University, which as you know is an open university. I am in charge of the B.A. program in history." Shiv pauses.

The girl gives him an encouraging nod. She looks at her notes, then asks, "Professor, what is your reaction to the charge that you have distorted historical facts?"

"I need to answer two questions here. One is regarding the charge. Who are the people making it, and are they qualified to recognize accepted historical facts. Or understand the nature of historical interpretation. Also, why they are bringing such a—" and a volcano erupts in the kitchen. The whooshy sound of escaping steam drowns Shiv's words.

"Cut," barks a man in the shadows. "Jasjit," calls the girl. Jasjit goes to the kitchen and emerges with a contrite Kamla. Shiv notices that she is dressed up in a shiny red nylon sari with matching beads. "It was only the pressure cooker," she explains. "I've switched off the stove now."

Back to the lights and camera. Shiv's nose itches. "Could you just take it from the middle," asks the girl. He doesn't dare tell her he has forgotten what he said.

"The important thing to remember," he says instead, "is that history, like the human mind, is a complex body with many strands. Ours is a rich, plural history. Of course all these threads must be repeatedly re-examined."

The girl looks blank but nods gamely.

Suddenly memory returns and Shiv locates some of the things he had planned to say. "But why this sudden anxiety about a historical figure we have safely consigned to textbooks till now? And from such unlikely quarters? I can only think of one answer—a fear of history. A fear that our history will force people to see that our past, like our present, has always had critics of social divisions that masquerade as religion and tradition. So what do these frightened people do? They whitewash historical figures, they seize history and restructure notions about—" and the lights go off. Someone in the darkness exhales with disgust.

An hour later, they are finally through. Or so Shiv thinks, but he is told he should continue to sit on his chair for some "filler" shots. "But all this for just three minutes?" he asks the girl, who looks as fresh as if she is in an air-conditioned studio. "We'll edit it," she promises, and though this explains nothing to Shiv, he leans back, resigned.

Meena emerges from her room and stands at the door, leaning on her crutch, watching. Shiv introduces the girl to her.

"Hi," the two of them say, each eyeing the other warily.

The mike is off, but Shiv feels stiff and self-conscious because he has been asked to "act naturally" for the camera. Acting naturally (for a history professor) apparently means a book in his lap, pretending to read, turning pages. Looking up thoughtfully at the ceiling as if he is his absentminded colleague Menon's clone. Though Shiv doesn't look at Meena, he can sense her suppressed laughter make its way to him across the floodlit room.

. . .

A haze of smoke hangs in Meena's room though Shiv has opened the windows and the door. He has a sense of having been here before: the smoky, dusty room, he on the periphery of the initiated circle, the selected few who can complete each other's sentences because they speak an exclusive language. Their sense of belonging, their confidence in the familiar ritual that holds them together, remind Shiv of his mother's marathon prayer sessions, the interminable pujas she held in her room to negotiate with the fates who were holding his father hostage. The same sense of expectation permeates the air now—that this time perhaps the tired old weapon may actually work.

Luckily Meena and Amar cannot see the heretical associations Shiv's memory is turning over. Amar's young band of warriors is in conference in Meena's room again, this time (in Amar's words) "to finalize a hard-hitting leaflet." This time Kamla is in the kitchen brewing tea, and Shiv is (as he was all those years ago in his mother's room) onlooker to others' campaign rituals.

Meena looks unbathed in the baggy gray T-shirt she wore to bed the night before. Her uncombed hair hangs in crazy rebellious curls to one side of her face. "Let me read out what we have so far," she is saying. "The protection racket is not a new one in some parts of the country. Shops, restaurants, hotels, factories, have all been, in the recent past, at the receiving end of protection—protection for a price. These instances of protection have also familiarized us with the protectors' preferred strategy. Convince people they are under attack. Then offer them protection."

Meena reads well. Despite the leg in the cast and her scruffy appearance today, her face glows in the smoky room, almost like an avenging angel's. Shiv finds himself drawn in. He promises himself he will not let his thoughts stray again; he reminds himself sharply that the meeting is about him, that it is *his* world at stake. His eyes fix on Meena.

"Consider the words of the Itihas Suraksha Manch leader who is offering to protect our history for us: 'Texts which overemphasize caste divisions and project the Hindu religion and Hindu culture in a poor light should not be allowed. Such conspiracies to tarnish the image of the Indian past should be met with courage. People feel free to revile Hinduism with impunity, but they do not dare criticize Islam because then the swords would be out.'

"Now consider the words written by a man who is the Manch's theoretical inspiration, if such as the Manch can be coupled with theory. Though now disowned and out of print, *We or the Nationhood Defined* by Madhav Sadashiv Golwalkar describes a past, a present and a future for India—a Hindu Rashtra: 'Foreign races in Hindusthan must either adopt the Hindu culture and language, learn to respect and hold in reverence the Hindu religion and must entertain no ideas but those of the glorification of the Hindu race and culture . . . or may stay in the country wholly subordinated to the Hindu nation.'"

Meena looks around triumphantly. "Sounds quite good, doesn't it? In the interest of peace and for the protection of . . . We need a few examples of all the times we have heard this in the last few years."

Amar immediately begins counting off on his fingers, "Campaigns against Christians, the murder of Australian missionary Graham Staines and his two children . . ."

"The attacks on artist M. F. Husain for painting Hindu goddesses in the nude," interrupts Meena, rolling her eyes to show what she thinks of both the goddesses and the attackers.

"Teachers in Goa having their faces blackened for setting 'politically incorrect' exams and the recall of a volume on the freedom struggle," adds Shiv, surprising them and himself. "The disruption of the shooting of a film on the plight of Hindu widows in Banaras."

"The list is endless," says Amar, "I think you have enough now, Meena. How are we going to end it?"

"I thought I'd use some of what you said on television," Meena says to Shiv. "Something about history not yet being a protected, endangered species. And I think it would be good to bring in the German fascists again, considering how much Golwalkar admired them. Jyoti, pass me that paragraph we drafted together."

She takes the piece of paper from Jyoti and reads to them: "One of the pictures history brings to mind at this juncture is that of a German town, storm troopers in brown shirts on the rampage. Perhaps we have not yet reached the pinnacle of atrocities committed during Kristallnacht, but it is impossible not to see a link. The link between fascism and the ugly faces of Hindutva unveiling themselves around us is the regimentation of thought and the brutal repression of culture."

Meena turns again to Shiv, a hundred-watt smile on her face. "What do you think? Does it sound alright?"

"Wonderful," says Shiv, meaning it. He has had a hard time recognizing his own words in what she read out, and there isn't a single word on Basava, but all the same Shiv finds it moving and frightening in equal measure.

"Well, that's just the leaflet," says Amar. "We have to come up with much more."

Meena turns back to him eagerly.

"Think of them as an army," Amar tells them. "The fundoo side has three regiments. The troops in front are the thugs. Lumpen types, rushing ahead with their prejudices like shields before them, waving hatred like angry lathis." Amar pauses a beat, allowing his images to hit their mark. "Then behind these you have the ideawallas. The historians, the ideologues. A few politicians and pamphleteers on the make. Bringing up the distant rear is the pantheon of gods in power. These think they should run the government because they have a direct line to the mythical gods."

The fundoo army has yet another man on the run. This may be news to the gods, but word has already got through to Seattle. Rekha is on the phone again, but she no longer seems to remember the existence of her precious garden, or the household, or even Meena. Her low, cool voice is pitched at a higher note than usual.

"I read the news online," she says. "Why didn't you tell me it was a bigger mess than I thought?"

"It just grew before I knew what was happening," Shiv says, on the defensive. But he also catches the bewilderment in her voice, the sense of disbelief he too has been feeling. "It's so sudden, so unexpected," he says. "The fuss, the interviews, being hated by people I don't even know . . . It's all strange and new—at least to me," he adds humbly.

Rekha listens in silence, then she says wearily, "I should get back, I can't stay on for another month. I'll worry too much about what will happen next if I am here. About how you are managing it all."

For an instant Shiv sees a tempting vision: Rekha in charge; and all the rest—the Head and the Dean, Meena and Amar, even the Manch and poison-ink *Current*—sent to their respective seats in a well-ordered classroom. Shiv regretfully lets go of this comforting illusion. "Let's not do anything in a hurry," he says. "I'm fine and there's nothing to manage. A lot of people—respected academics—are supporting me. In any case, the lesson has gone to some review panel of supposed experts."

Rekha sighs in exasperation. "I wish you hadn't got involved in something like this. And all for a correspondence course and some poet no one remembers. It's so unlike you too."

"These phone calls are getting expensive," says Shiv. "I'll e-mail you every time I go to the Department. Or I'll buy a modem for the old computer at home. Anyway, don't do anything to your ticket yet—maybe it will fizzle out soon—go away as suddenly as it came. Maybe we're making too much of a little thing."

Shiv himself does not believe this for a minute. If anything, he can sense something, a whole series of events designed to take him by surprise, waiting in the wings. Brewing while waiting to catch him unprepared. But how is he to prepare if he doesn't really know what the other side might do?

The only thing he can think of is to go back to his lesson, or study his notes on Basava; prepare for cross-examination by strangers, whether on the other side or his own. Shiv has heard the subtext of Rekha's words. A poet no one remembers. What she means is, what difference does it make? Whatever he said and did, he is dead and gone, and you are here and alive.

Rekha has never understood the pleasures, or the uses, of speculation. The first few times he spoke to her of his father—of what may have happened to him so that he disappeared—Rekha listened to him with sympathy. She lost patience when she saw that his father's ghost refused to be exorcised; when she saw that he refused to leave, or, more accurately, that Shiv refused to let him go. "What's the use of beating it to death when you can't possibly know for sure?" she asked him sharply when she heard him go over that "last day" again and again, painfully piecing together fact and supposition.

But all that was a long time ago. It's been years now since his father was mentioned between them. His father still remains, though; he is there between them like a secretive past that grows heavier every day. And now Basava, the other mystery Rekha would like to safely banish to an irrelevant past. Basava, a man of his times, but also a man whose *questions* remain relevant eight hundred years later. Basava was no cardboard saint singing syrup-sweet devotional songs, only concerned with the hereafter. For a brief period, probably the span of one generation, Basava helped create a new community; a new ethos, that provoked people to *dare* to experiment.

What happened, finally, to this man? Though Shiv has read whatever he can lay his hands on about Basava's life, his end remains a mystery. It is this mystery that Shiv finds himself going back to again and again; the point at which Basava leaves the city and the collapsing movement, and returns to Kudalasangama, the confluence of rivers where he began his career.

Basava's death will always have a resonance for Shiv. A special message he must decode though he does not know how to go about it.

Each of us carries within ourselves a history, an encyclopedia of images, a landscape with its distinct patterns of mutilation. A dictionary that speaks the languages of several pasts, that moves across borders, back and forth between different times. Some biographers date Basava's death—or the presumption of death—as January 1168. But in Shiv's mind, this tentative date creeps forward insidiously. Not to June 7, 1962, when his father disappeared, but to its medieval counterpart, June 7, 1168.

Like Shiv's father, Basava disappeared. He was presumed dead. His end would always be shrouded by mysterious circumstances and speculation. Speculative narratives. Narratives of love or faith or revolution. But is all narrative doomed to be inconclusive?

All Shiv knows is that Basava left his home, his family, his city. He went back to Sangama, tired, disillusioned with his old friend and ally King Bijjala, perhaps with his own colleagues as well. A man close to the end, looking back to the past, remembering, evaluating, settling accounts. Trying to understand what had gone wrong. Trying to mine this failure for new answers to old questions. Living out, perhaps, a full day of reckoning, a life in a day, on June 7, 1168. There he was, a man by the river, the images of the past (credit, debit, profit, loss) a watery parade passing before him.

Now, more than ever, Shiv feels the need to construct a viable narrative of that last day, the key to a life. The narrative is speculative, fragmentary; but with the ghost of Basava—or his father—standing behind him, egging him on, Shiv's imagination travels beyond the modest limits of prescribed module and syllabus. It begins, appropriately, with daybreak, with the tentative but hopeful light of sunrise over the river. There is a temple in the background, a whitewashed temple glistening like a silver signal. But the temple is not important for the moment. Shiv looks into the frame, zooming in on the man who stands alone by the river.

Shiv has only seen Basava's pictures in the style of calendar art, but these images are forgettable, unlike the photographs he has seen of his father. So Shiv's Basava, the man by the river: he is sixty two but there is not a single wrinkle on his deep-brown face. His hair is still thick. From a distance it is all black, an unruly, wavy bush. Close up, the bush glints with silver strands, almost a decorative touch. His face is usually smooth-shaven, but now there is soft stubble on his chin and upper lip. This mossy unkempt stubble on his chin softens the sharp edge of his face about the jaw. For someone who has worn elegant silk all his years in the court (simple fabric, quiet colors, but silk all the same), he is now almost naked. A modest-sized white cloth is tied about his hips; the same rough-textured sort that made up his entire wardrobe in his youth by this river. The cloth is clean but damp; the outline of the loincloth below is clearly visible. There is not an ounce of flab on him; he is not a tall man or a particularly well-built one. The overall impression is of a fine, economically etched figure, with neat, functioning muscles and a straight spine firmly perpendicular to the ground he stands on. Hardness in miniature. A modest-sized, modestly dressed middle-aged man with large warrior-eyes. His eyes, where his power resides, now twin mirrors of the river.

Shiv tries to understand this river, Basava's powerful river. It is a river that never stands still. It keeps moving, this river, flowing day after day, night after night. What can a river do but flow? From a distance, it is just a simple body of water, mindlessly acting out its nature, its constant movement a quest without a purpose. But close up, all complacent assumptions of simplicity vanish. There is nothing obvious about this river. Nothing about this river is what it seems. Close up, the river is actually two rivers. Two rivers flowing down their separate courses, then meeting, parting; meeting, parting, till they come to a point of union, a union deep enough for them to emerge flowing as a composite third river.

Shiv sees Basava standing by the river, considering it with a mixture of love and wariness as if he can see truth in the river. Truth, that large map of abstraction so many men fight over, die for, is the size of a pinpoint—just a glimmer in a drop of water, part of the flowing stream. And what is this truth Basava sees in the river? That crosscurrents can coexist, that rapids and the most placid of waters are fellow travelers? Or that it is possible to move, to break free of gold-encrusted temples, customs and prejudices made of petrified stone, aspiring to stand like monuments for all time?

SEVEN

SEPTEMBER 18–23

*I*n another time, on another day, Basava and his river are exchanging subtleties on the nature of many-faceted truth. In September 2000, as Shiv sits in his room in the university's History Department, Basava could well be on another planet. A Martian saint-poet.

Shiv has come to the Department to meet the Head, but all he wants is to sit alone in his room. All he wants to do is take down books from his bookshelf, find the right references, and begin writing a new lesson. He wants to go back to being a simple teacher. Go back to that essential process of collating salient facts and bringing it all together in some meaningful shape. He wants to recapture for a moment the experience of a creator, or at least a quasi creator, of a design. Only that will make him feel at home in this room again. Make him feel it is indeed his, that he has a right to it.

Though he is faceless to the readers of his lessons, Shiv too felt the urgency of a teacher at one time, when he still had a real classroom. Later this urge to make someone understand what he had to say came upon him in fits and starts, usually when Rekha and he went for an evening walk. But he soon learnt to rein in that urge, what Rekha calls his attacks of professoritis. The irony is that it is now, when he coordinates resources for educational clients, when he no longer has a student walking shoulder to shoulder with him, that he is being tried, and displayed, as a real, living teacher.

Shiv tries to read the pile of papers in his In-tray, mark time before he sees the Head. But the memos and notices, all the boring, reassuring signposts of normalcy, are written in some indecipherable language. A foreign tongue. He puts them aside and looks out of the window; his recent conversation with Menon comes to mind. Menon, the sort of academic who feels safest in a maze of files, records and rules, called Shiv this morning to add a new anxiety to his hoard. "Shiv, you're lucky all this is happening in Delhi," said Menon. "You know how people here have trouble remembering what has happened in the rest of the country."

Shiv waited patiently; Menon does not take kindly to being hurried out of his maze.

"It seems there was a similar controversy in 1994. But that was about a play on Basava, and the play was written in Kannada. Do you know anything about this?"

Since the call, as if the file in Shiv's mind has just been waiting for Menon to open it, he has remembered. (It shocks Shiv that he, who prides himself on his good memory, has not recalled this in the past weeks of confusion.)

The play Menon was talking about was published in 1986.

It won a state award and was prescribed as a textbook in a couple of universities. Then eight years later, some group in Karnataka—cousins, or ancestors, of Shiv's Manch—woke up to the possibilities of the book. They accused the play of portraying Basava as a coward; implying that he committed suicide; casting aspersions on the "chastity" of some women saints; and letting some characters use obscene language.

The group demanded that the play be withdrawn from the university syllabus. There were the usual ban-the-book scenes. Copies were burnt; so was an effigy of the playwright. Rallies were held for and against; buses and trains came to a halt. There were protest fasts; one man attempted self-immolation. Most of all, it became a convenient election issue. Finally, "in view of the law and order situation" the book was withdrawn from the university syllabus in 1995 by government order.

Now, in 2000, the distance between the imaginary lands of literature and the prosaic city of history has shrunk. All occupy the same beleaguered space, the same territory under indefinite siege. The horizon, the sky, all wide-open spaces are reduced to the size of a pinpoint; the Manch and its cohorts are telling them all that there is only one way to remember a great man, *their* way. Only one way to remember the past.

Perhaps Shiv would be better off if he allowed his memory to be sullied; if he remembered less, if he turned his back on his father's ideal historian. If he allowed a simple excision of memory, a few minor assaults on shade, nuance, complexity. But will he recover? Or will he skulk around the rest of his life, a paid witness, a hireling of thugs?

As if she knows Shiv is cornered, that he is casting about for refuge, Meena wanders into his mind. Meena sitting straight in bed, her cast stretched before her, every muscle of her body tense, an alert healthy animal ready to pounce. Meena sitting among her friends, girl-matriarch, listening to Amar proposing leaflets, posters, a "broad-front" rally.

She is just twenty-four. At an age when she should be looking at love for the first time, trembling with wonder and confusion at the mysteries of the human heart. The human body, her own body. A man's body.

Instead she sits in a meeting to rescue an aging historian from the mob. Her eyes fill with yearning, but it is not a desire Shiv has seen in a woman's face before. Meena's fish-eyes, made for poetry, yearn to look a starker terror in the face. They do not flinch at the prospect of violence, of violation. They wait, with a youthful certainty Shiv finds unbearable, to meet halfway some brutal, premeditated injury, the very opposite of love.

Her brief history, a history of doing. His longer history, peopled with events in books, bound to a repository of public events long past. Now, after long safe years, the custodian is being shown the door.

In the days when Shiv was on the crossroads to manhood, there were only three professions open—or so it seemed to his uncle, his surrogate father. Doctor, engineer, chartered accountant. Anything else was out of the question. Teaching was not beyond the pale, as business was, for example. But to choose teaching was also an admission of failure, a regressive choice of dubious, impractical virtue.

Shiv's daughter, Tara, always an indifferent student, now has some sort of job in America to do with computers. Her salary—a clear indication that Rekha's genes have triumphed over his—would have assured his uncle that Shiv's existence is justified. Shiv wonders now about Tara: how well does he really know her? She is younger than Meena, but unlike her, Tara couldn't wait to finish with life as a student. Her world is a small, small place, but she knows it very well indeed. Delhi to Seattle via computer courses, competitive exams, a job that promises a yuppie future. Tara seems to have entirely escaped Shiv's fumbling, yearning uncertainties, his hole-in-the-soul sense of being incomplete. Tara overcame doubt very early in her life. Shiv remembers the time when she was seven or eight, a plump, neat little girl. She sought him out in his study and told him, with all the confidence of a conformist bent on survival, "My teacher and my friends say there's a god. The whole world says it; only you say there isn't a god. I'll believe the whole world, not you."

It's the same easy belief that makes Tara e-mail Shiv now: I've been getting messages from friends in Delhi and some Indians here. It's sort of weird and embarrassing to explain why you have written something against our temples and priests and all that. It's only after coming to the US that many of us have learnt to appreciate Indian traditions. This sounds like a lecture, doesn't it, and that must amuse you, considering I always ran away from your lectures!

At the bottom of Tara's message is a line that has recently begun to border all her e-mail. The exact words change from time to time, but they are all variations on the same theme: Joy, peace and love—may these blessings find their way to you. Below this sweet if impractical thought is the ubiquitous question, Do you yahoo?

The phone rings and Shiv looks at his watch. Fifteen minutes to go for his meeting with the Head. He picks up the phone.

"Dr. Murthy?" asks Mrs. Khan. "The Head would like to speak to you."

Shiv holds on to the receiver and listens to two different pitches of static on the line, two incompatible tracks playing simultaneously.

"Dr. Murthy," the Head's voice echoes Mrs. Khan's greeting with false heartiness. "How are you?"

Shiv is not sure this merits a reply, but the Head is rushing ahead anyway. "I'm sorry, I can't squeeze in our meeting after all. I have to leave in a minute for an emergency meeting across the city—and you know how the office-hour traffic is. But I thought I would quickly bring you up-to-date. Just think it out carefully, Shiv. You know I want you to continue in our Department. And I'm sorry the lesson had to be recalled—but these things happen, it's all part of the game. The best thing now would be to keep quiet. Wait for the storm to blow over. I must tell you the Dean and I are distressed that you are talking to the media. It's your decision, but if I were you, I would be more cautious."

The car sent by the studio is plush and air-conditioned. With the distance to be covered, and the traffic en route, Shiv is safe in this cool, silent, moving island for what seems a lifetime. The untidy, grasping tentacles of Delhi are outside the window glass, powerless. They seem to belong to a television program, to a viewer's guide to some distant, seething planet. Thank god, you think, watching the images on the screen-like window glass, that I don't live in a place like that.

When the car turns into the studio compound and comes to a halt, he is reluctant to emerge. If he gets out of the car, he will have to let go of his hour of limbo, with someone else doing the driving, to parts of the city he has never seen before. He will have to let go of the illusion of being mid-journey, of many long, safe hours before he goes back to being himself.

In the studio building, Shiv is met by a young woman in jeans and a T-shirt. A mobile phone grows out of her hand like an unshapely wart. She ushers Shiv into what appears to be a dentist's waiting room. Two or three bored occupants, reading dog-eared back issues of magazines, look up the instant they walk in. "I'll send in some tea and biscuits," the woman promises and disappears. The others, having exhausted the brief distracting possibilities of examining Shiv, go back to their magazines.

A while later, the mobile-woman returns. "You can go to the makeup room now," she tells Shiv. "One of the other panelists is already there." (Shiv knows, from the way she says this, that this is a bigwig, an in-favor government-type.) "I hope you don't mind sharing the makeup room."

As she speaks, the woman opens a door, sticks her head in and says, "Sultan, I've brought the professor*ji* for makeup." She leaves Shiv to Sultan's mercy and shuts the door behind her.

The room is small and brilliantly lit. It is entirely lined with mirrors on one side. The room itself seems to be all corners. It is almost triangular, and the lights and mirrors combine to multiply corners—real corners and mirror-corners. There are two chairs with armrests and headrests before the mirror.

The bigwig is in one of the chairs. His bushy eyebrows rise a fraction at the sight of Shiv in the other chair. Just a fraction but that is enough for his eyebrows to meet the outward-growing bush on his head. The bridge of skin in between collapses and disappears entirely, making way for two continents of hair to meet and merge.

The makeup man, Sultan, is one of those men who has taken stock of the place he has to work in and adapted himself to it. He is so thin that his features flatten out obediently into a straight line every time he presents himself in profile. But he makes up for his insubstantial appearance with his hospitable air. "Just a minute, sir. I'll be with you in a minute," he says to Shiv. Or to Shiv's reflection. (All conversation in this room is held with reflections, with the makeup man behind whoever is in the makeup chair.)

Shiv sees Sultan's reflection hovering round the bigwig's bushy face, brush and sponge to hand. The bigwig's face turns an even, unhealthy pink. He shuts his eyes with a sigh, as if used to catching a nap on the move.

A few minutes later, Sultan is done. The bigwig opens his eyes and blinks at the pink mask in the mirror. He examines the blush painted on his face, then yawns. Shiv can see the bigwig's thick gray tongue in the mirror. Though it lies still in his mouth like a sleepy, fat slug, Shiv suspects it is usually agile and darting. The bigwig gets up and bustles out of the room. Sultan comes over to Shiv, smiling shyly. "Now sir, let me see what I can do for you," he says.

The mobile-woman returns just as Sultan releases Shiv from the room of mirrors. "Ready, sir?" she asks, and leads the way. Armed with pancake, his thinning hair artfully combed to fool the general public, he follows her to where the cameras wait.

She pushes open a door with a sign that says No Entry; there is also a red light blinking above the door for those who require more than one warning. A blast of air-conditioning greets them as they step into a cavern-like room, all the lights directed at a semicircular table.

"The show is a straightforward panel discussion," the mobile-woman tells Shiv. "There are two panelists other than you, and the moderator—" She breaks off as the host of the program comes toward them. Shiv notices that the bigwig is one of the other panelists. He is looking at Shiv avidly, a hawk waiting to swoop down on a delectable mouse.

Much later in the day, his face washed of pancake, Shiv tells Meena about the bigwig's version of Basava's story. He had, to Shiv's surprise, done some homework. But predictably, his homework on Basava and his times refused to go beyond legends and tales. He recounted, in shrewd politician-style, some rosy myths about Basava's divine powers.

"Apparently Basava was not human from the very beginning," Shiv tells Meena. "We had to hear a long and involved story about the cosmic events that led to Siva sending his bull to earth as Basava. He sent his bull to earth because"—Shiv mimes derisive quotation marks—"of the unfortunate status of devotion on earth. So, the bigwig went on to ask, What was the difficulty in Basava's escaping death, of his 'shedding his mortal coils' and going back to Siva when his earthly mission was accomplished?"

The bigwig had also stumbled upon one of the more peculiar examples of Basava's supposed miracles. There has been some speculation about who fathered Basava's nephew, the veerashaiva leader Chennabasava. "The bigwig had done enough homework to find the best explanation," says Shiv. "It seems Basava was praying when he saw an ant hurrying along with a seed in its mouth. Basava took this seed for some reason and gave it to his sister Nagamma, and the result was an immaculate conception."

Meena laughs uproariously.

"Have you ever noticed," she says to Shiv, "how close some of these mythical explanations are to the small print on official documents? I mean, you can really see the governmentwallas in these convoluted myths, bending over backwards to do some damage control."

Shiv is losing count of interviews, meetings, telephone calls. Meena has forgotten about her itchy knee. She sits in her bed, phone in hand, a general on the battlefield directing operations. The occasional awkward silence that would sit between them in the early days is now filled; they have more than enough to talk about, all safe subjects. But sometimes, Shiv finds himself shutting out her voice. He looks at her instead. At her eyes. Into her eyes, the tumultuous place where Meena lives.

Then her voice intrudes into his daydream. "Shiv?" she says sharply. "What do you think—did you hear what I said?"

He shakes his head, but his heart, an absurd and frivolous creature, grows light and buoyant. It's the first time she has called him by name. And as always with Meena, it is a natural act, performed entirely without self-consciousness.

Then the doorbell rings. The telephone wakes up. Professional hatemongers pen letters to the editor.

Dear Sir,

It is high time our so-called historians presented Hinduism and its famous tolerance in its true light. This Professor Murthy has made the great saint Basavanna a mere politician, appeal-

ing to caste and dividing society just like Mandal did some years back. Maybe the esteemed Professor needs a refresher course in more recent history? When the Pope came to India, he refused to apologize for Christian conversions, yet he was treated to Hindu hospitality. As for Islam, its advent might have been a boon for the Arabs who united under its banner, but it has been a curse for people outside the Arab world. Wherever the Islamic hordes went, they conquered, killed and plundered. The Islamic belief that political power can be claimed by anyone who can wield the sword goes against the legality of inheritance to the throne. It also encourages intrigues, plots, rebellions and assassinations of father by son, brother by brother, ruler by military commander or minister, and above all, master by servant, nay, even by slave.

Our misled historians and other troublemakers criticize Hinduism for its caste system and pull our saints off their pedestals. But they keep quiet about Christianity or Islam. The truth is that these minorities will be safe in India only if they share our vision of our country and culture. Then we won't mind accommodating two more gods (Allah and Christ) along with our three hundred and thirty million gods and goddesses.

Yours, etc.,
Prof. (Shri) M. M. Behoshi
(failed Oxon, 1942)

Meena throws the newspaper aside as if it is infectious. "I wonder what your colleagues are doing," she says to Shiv. "I know your wimpy Head is avoiding you, but what about the rest of them? Can they be persuaded to take a stand—come out and say something against the Manch and the Head and whatshisname? The Department fundoo?"

"Arya," says Shiv. The word slips out of his mouth so easily. It is so light, this easily said two-syllable name. It rises into the air above them like a spiral of smoke detaching itself from the reality below, the man with the ugly fire raging inside him. And Arya brings to mind the rest of the core faculty. Just three weeks back Shiv was still a member of the clan, sharing their daily concerns and their boredom and those interminable cups of venomous Department tea. But now, with Shiv marked as a creature apart, a foreigner like Mrs. Khan, the core faculty may as well be complete strangers to him. A secret society that speaks an exotic, excluding language. "I spoke to Menon, he was telling me about a somewhat similar case—"

"You'll have to meet them all, Shiv," interrupts Meena. "You can't avoid a confrontation, you have to get the Head to meet all of you." She pauses, her face taking on a hungry, expectant look that reminds Shiv of the predatory bigwig in the studio. "Even better, you have to confront this Arya. Ignoring him is not going to make him go away."

The telephone rings. Meena picks it up immediately. "Yes, I'm Meena," she says. "Oh, I'm fine." Whoever is on the phone obviously has a lot to say. Meena looks at Shiv, her face stretched into a comical mask of mock-dismay, her eyes lit with amusement. "No, I don't know when the cast will come off," she now says. "Shiv is here, he'll talk to you. Just a second."

She covers the mouthpiece with her hand and says to Shiv in a teasing, exaggerated whisper. "Phew! Someone called Amita Sen. Very sweet and ladylike, ve-ry concerned about my leg though she has never set eyes on me. She has to talk to you *urgently.* Special friend of yours, eh?" She grins at him with wicked shrewdness as she hands him the phone. Shiv takes it, flustered and guilty, as if it is Rekha in the room with him, not Meena.

Amita is in full flow. "I'm so glad she's better—your ward I mean—her name is Meena, isn't it? She sounds very young. But Shiv, I'm calling so we can meet today, I have so much to tell you. Let's meet somewhere quiet, away from the campus."

"I don't know," Shiv begins, but Amita hastens to add, "Menon's coming too. We are both free today, and we've got to talk about what's happening, we have to figure out how Menon and I can help. You know we are on your side, don't you, Shiv?"

Shiv is on the road again, but this time he is not floating in limbo, safe in an anonymous studio vehicle. He is driving his own Maruti, feeling like a child who has stolen out of the house without his guardian's approval. Meena does not know where he is going; though Menon will be there too, he couldn't bring himself to tell her he is going to meet Amita. Amita did not say what exactly she and Menon have in mind, and Shiv was anxious to cut short her call. But he is sure they plan more than reassurance and sympathy over lunch; Menon at least must have some plan for a meeting at the Department.

If he had not been so secretive, Shiv thinks, if he had told Meena that he is meeting his colleagues outside the campus, she would probably have been delighted. "To chalk out a plan?" she would have asked. Shiv's car makes a furtive, steady sound as if humming under its breath. For a moment, he feels a childish thrill: if he is up to a clandestine meeting, or at least a little plotting against the Head, he must still be in control of his life. He eases the pressure of his foot on the accelerator and crawls to a halt at an intersection.

The traffic lights are not working. All around him, cars, buses, autos, scooters, cycles and pedestrians compete with each other, determined to go ahead before the traffic on the other side gets there first. The air fills with impatient honking. Shiv wills himself to wait, to remain the rule-following person he thinks he is.

He waits. He shuts out the noise around him by pretending he is in the middle of a silent movie. Chaos in silence, chaos more easily managed. The city looks more squalid than usual somehow, an exhibitionist showing off its open wounds. Surely some of these gaping potholes are new? The ugly pockmarked buildings on either side of the road sit watching the commuters like an unhappy, unwilling audience.

Then Shiv sees the woman and her companion. The young woman is hugely pregnant; her midriff is bare between her blouse and skirt. The companion is an old woman wizened with worry. Together they dodge their way between the restless cars as they try one driver after the other. Even before they come closer Shiv can see their taut, desperate faces: he saw them last month with exactly the same expression. Back then, as he waited at these same traffic lights, the two women went begging for help from car to car. The young woman moaned, her face contorted with pain. Her hands held the dangerously low bulge in such a way that Shiv's own stomach lurched with sympathy. The light turned green. Shiv opened his wallet quickly and gave a couple of the notes to the older woman. Then he put his car into gear with an apologetic look.

Now, a month later, still at the same place, the two women are working their way toward him. The young one is still pregnant. She moves slowly as if her baby will be born any minute. They have reached the car to his left. Shiv can't believe he is seeing the same scene again; he also feels his muscles tense as if he is watching a tightrope act.

The man in the car to the left stares ahead, intent on the traffic. But there is a bus before him and he cannot pretend to inch forward. He looks at the women sheepishly, then pulls out his wallet. Shiv wants to switch off the engine, get out of his car and say to them as if he has gone backstage after a performance, Bravo! The women turn toward his car. Their eyes meet Shiv's; all three of them are trapped together in a few seconds of piercing clarity; then the women scuttle away.

The honking reaches a frenzied pitch. The lights are back; the traffic is moving with a vengeance to make up for lost time. A truck snorts as it rushes past Shiv. Its exhaust smoke hangs in the air for a moment as if it does not know where to go.

The restaurant Amita has picked turns out to be the sort that is dimly lit so it can pretend the air-conditioning is more potent than it is. But Shiv feels energized somehow by his encounter with the women on the road. It was a brief holiday from his troubles, this glimpse of others' desperate survival strategies.

But when he tells Amita and Menon about the professionally pregnant woman—and he does this right away, he can't bear to begin on his own business yet—he is amazed by their reaction. "Shouldn't believe every sob story you hear," Menon says disapprovingly, then falls silent as if he has said too much. Amita is more voluble. "How could you, Shiv, how could you get fooled so easily? I can't believe you actually gave her money the last time. How much did you give her? You should have taken them to the police station today."

Shiv is actually relieved when the conversation moves to the inevitable, waiting track. The Department, the Head, Shiv's options. He is also taken aback—when she spoke to him on the phone, Amita did not let on about the minor miracle she and Menon have already managed: an "extraordinary" faculty meeting to be held in the Department.

"I never thought Menon could be so tough," Amita gushes, her voice shrill with newfound admiration. "The Head didn't know what hit him." She chuckles, leaning toward Menon and blowing a cloud of cigarette smoke into his face. "Just goes to show, doesn't it—you think you know a person you've been seeing day after day, then suddenly, like magic, the person surprises you."

Menon winces and passes Amita the chicken; she obediently puts out her cigarette and serves herself. Menon may be less effusive than Amita, but Shiv can hear the quiet satisfaction in his voice. "The meeting's on," he says. "The Head must have seen he can't avoid a faculty meeting indefinitely. Arya will be there, of course, and he's bound to make a nuisance of himself." Menon pauses, then goes on with an air of confessing something, "But Arya actually helped me engineer the meeting, can you imagine? He pressurized the Head even more than I did. So let's hope for the best."

Shiv enters the room and feels a strange sense of letdown. Everything is as banal and predictable as usual: the dusty, cobwebbed room, the temperamental tubelight, the curtains faded an indeterminate gray. The core faculty gathered in the inevitable room, every one of them including the Head, Mrs. Khan to hand with the ubiquitous pad and pen. All is as usual, and Shiv automatically makes his way to the empty chair beside Amita.

But once he has sat down, looked around, he sees the little paradox he has missed. The cast remains the same, yet it is not unchanged. Not one of them is really at ease. All is not as usual: Shiv sees this now, in the stiff, self-conscious way they sit in their chairs, waiting anxiously to play out unfamiliar, unscripted roles. And as if to remind him that this is an extraordinary meeting with no time for frivolous distractions, the usual tea is missing. Shiv catches Mrs. Khan's eye; she gives him a brief, watery smile, then looks away.

The Head frowns at her. "I don't think we need minutes today, Mrs. Khan," he says, nodding his head censoriously at her pad. "This is just an informal meeting with Dr. Murthy." So, Shiv thinks, the swine wants to settle it all off the record. He steels himself.

But it is Arya who puts the Head in place. "I don't know why we are pretending there is no problem. I suggest"—and he leers at the cowering Mrs. Khan—"every word spoken today, any explanation Dr. Murthy may have to offer us, should be on record." Shiv turns to Arya with distaste. The man's face looks bloated as if he has been feasting on Shiv's misery. Shiv's eyes move to Menon and they exchange a speaking look. No wonder Arya was an unexpected accomplice; he wanted the meeting so he could gloat in public over the Manch's new victim.

"Well," says the Head, looking miserable. "Take the minutes down, Mrs. Khan, but show me what you have written once it is typed. We'll have to decide whether it should go on file then." It's impossible not to feel sorry for the Head; obviously nothing in his career has prepared him to take on intimidation by the likes of Arya and his goons.

Now the Head valiantly tries to hold his own. "We might as well get to the point. The point is that the Department and the University are doing their level best to defuse this crisis before it gets completely out of hand." He nods at Mrs. Khan who is writing down every pearl of wisdom. "As you know, the lesson has been sent to an expert committee for a fair, balanced review. Meanwhile it's best perhaps that Dr. Murthy—"

"But do we know who these experts are?" Amita asks bravely. Shiv gives her a grateful look and takes the plunge. "If the Manch is satisfied with this committee, the chances are the committee does not have a single historian we can take seriously. And what about the precedent we are setting? With the lesson and with the 'suggestion' for my resignation?"

Clearly the Head did not expect Shiv to get to the matter so quickly or to put it all so bluntly. After all, he handpicked Shiv for the Department, counting on his being a cautious, reliable team worker.

But again, it is Arya who speaks up before the Head. "The Manch represents public sentiment. History and everything else should respect this. For years leftist and pseudosecular historians have been filling committees with their agents. Now their monopoly is over and they are making a hue and cry."

"I never claimed to be a Marxist, Dr. Arya," says Shiv, and the Head chips in with, "Yes, I can assure you Dr. Murthy's no communist. Whatever our little differences," he adds, reluctant to give Shiv a completely clean bill of health.

But Arya cannot be fobbed off so easily. There is the right side and there is the other side—whether these are Muslims or communists or Christians is all the same to him. As it is he is so agitated he can barely sit still. He looks as if he is ready to produce some instant hue and cry of his own.

Menon says with admirable calm, "Dr. Arya, there's no point getting emotional. We are supposed to be talking about a history lesson, and we can't have a discussion if we start drawing battle lines like this."

Arya glares at Menon, then at the Head. The Head does not look enthusiastic about this cue, but manages to say without looking anyone in the eye, "I may not put it like Dr. Arya, but I can understand why he is upset. We do need to talk about this lesson's implications. The question is, if our young people lose all sense of veneration for rishis, sages and saints, who should they look up to?"

"Michael Jackson?" pipes up his yes-man Dr. Kishan Lal who has been a quiet little mouse so far. "McDonald's culture with potatoes fried in beef tallow?"

The meeting is going nowhere. It's clear that whatever Amita, Menon and Shiv say, the result will be a stalemate. Mrs. Khan, who looks like she may burst into tears any minute, has abandoned her minutes. She mumbles an excuse about returning soon and leaves the room, shutting the door behind her. The Head looks after her longingly.

But Shiv is finally getting angry. He snaps at Lal, "This is precisely the danger of pandering to any self-appointed preservers of culture. What about—" and he finds himself being lifted off the floor. Arya has pounced on him and has him by the collar. Shiv can feel Arya's pungent breath on his face.

Menon too has jumped up and he is holding Arya round his waist, pulling him back.

"Dr. Arya," croaks the Head somewhere behind them. He has broken into a sweat and is panting as if he will have a heart attack any minute. "Please, let's remember we are in the University, not on the street."

Arya lets go of Shiv reluctantly and shakes off Menon. Amita rushes to Shiv to check that he is all right.

Suddenly Arya decides he's had enough; the day's mission has been accomplished. He goes to the door, then turns around for a parting shot. "If it comes to defending books by . . . who is it . . . Taslima Rushdie," he says. "If it is someone like that or someone who wants to make a hundred percent blue film about widows in Benares, the secular fundamentalists are all on the streets shouting No ban, no censorship. But our historians and thinkers and activists get different treatment. They won't even let us speak."

Arya's face promises Shiv they will meet once more. Then the door bangs shut and the meeting breaks up.

EIGHT

SEPTEMBER 25–30

Shiv is back in his room at the Department on Monday. The door is shut. He is tempted to switch off the light and fan as well so that no one knows he is here. But he stops short of such cowardice; besides, he finds he can't move from his chair. He sits there, empty-handed, listening to the pigeons making scrabbling noises on the cooler. He doesn't have the heart to chase them away today. Instead he shuts out their presence, looks out of the other window.

The view of the parking lot, a bland view that has met Shiv's eyes in so many moments of boredom and impatience, is comforting. Its loyal, unchanging features reassure him; the world outside the window is not—or not yet—a complete stranger. He counts four little Marutis including his own. Two Zens. A brave and battered old Fiat. And to one corner, a great big foreign-looking monster he can't identify, glinting ostentatiously in the sunlight.

Shiv has escaped here for an hour or two of silence. To be completely alone, to try and think dispassionately. The telephone receiver is off the hook. He thinks of Rekha's yoga instructor telling her to empty her mind of all thoughts but one. Hold the one lone fragment firmly in view till it grows bigger and stronger, filling the frame. The Head, the Dean, Amar and his band, even Arya's promise of more trouble to come, tumble out of Shiv's head. Meena, weighed down by her cast, is less willing to move. He shakes his head to clear it and fix its sights on his father.

This is an old habit; every time Shiv asks himself a question, it is his father who is the audience in his head. His reader, his fellow-questioner, his quiet but critical listener.

Shiv now asks himself (or his father): What makes a fanatic? A fundamentalist? What makes communities that have lived together for years suddenly discover a latent hatred for each other?

As if in answer, Shiv hears a distant rumble, then the parking lot fills with people. Even at a distance he can sense the tension in them, bodies like clenched fists, voices angry and shrill.

Shiv gets up slowly, deliberately, as if any sudden movement might break a bone. He moves to the window in a dream, in a hypnotic trance of horrified fascination. He has never seen so many students on this campus before. Then one of them looks up, catches his staring eye. In that instant of recognition, Shiv knows he is not a student. He remembers that it's the easiest thing in the world to hire protesters. All it takes is the price of a meal. Hungry touts are unlikely to ask what they are protesting against. They are also unlikely to shy away from violence.

The mob. A mob for Shiv, his own private adversary running him to earth.

There is a knock on the door and almost immediately the door is pushed open. It is Menon. The sight of him fills Shiv with gratitude. Menon must have known Shiv was here, yet he has left him alone. Shiv resolves never again to complain about Menon's lack of social skills.

"Shiv, what are you standing there for? Come on, you should leave from the back before they come up here."

They hear the flapping of wings on an ascending note. The pigeons have taken off. Abruptly, Shiv's trance lets go of him; his body comes back to life.

Menon and Shiv rush out of the room and dash down the stairs. When they get to the parking lot, it's empty.

At the car, Shiv turns to Menon. "I don't feel right about this. Why don't you call the security people? I could try and talk to the protesters till they come."

"I've already called the security," Menon says, and takes the car keys from Shiv. When he notices how unsteady Menon's hand is as he unlocks the door, Shiv's desire, for either dialogue or confrontation, dissipates.

He gets into the car and Menon slams the door shut.

Shiv sees Menon hurrying out of the frame in his rearview mirror. He starts the car, turns it around so it is facing his room. Then, in the empty lot, a parting shot reaches home, though Shiv is physically untouched. A chair flies out of the window of his room. A shower of glass follows, and papery confetti. Shiv pulls out of the parking lot, his foot pressed firmly on the accelerator. He races away from his room, the sight of its being stripped naked. Of its being turned into a sullied place, no longer anyone's refuge.

His room has been pushed into no-man's-land. Like other disputed structures, it has a padlock on the door. All it takes, it
appears, is a simple little lock to keep history safe.

Shiv tries to picture his ransacked room. He has not
been back, but Menon has told him that the table and chairs
and bookshelves are broken, the walls defaced. There are torn
books everywhere, cupboard and files open-mouthed and in
shambles. A jumble of crumpled paper. His nameplate is on
the floor in a heap of little pieces, like a jigsaw puzzle that will
need patience and imagination to put together again. And the
pigeons? wonders Shiv. He has hated those noisy, dirty birds
all these years, conducted warfare on them. But now the
thought of his room without the pigeons at the window makes
him feel bereft. Are they back? Or have they been scared away
for good?

Now that Arya and his cronies have made sure he cannot go
back to the Department, Shiv is a full-time fugitive. House-
bound, his own home feels like exile. And the inevitable flurry
of reactions has set in—phone calls, meetings, newly set up
committees. ("We suggest a committee be set up to constitute a
committee . . .") At the same time, Shiv's desecrated room is
being pushed into the background; even as he tries to keep it in
focus, it blurs, turning into history. What remains, what takes
over, is the aftermath—what the enemy will do next; and where
(and how) the argumentative battalion of soldiers on his side
will march together.

Shiv feels like a body that has been taken over. A body in a
lawless country, a body that has somehow unlearnt the law of
gravity. There is a sense of surging ahead, of careening; of the
wheel having taken over from the hand steering it. Every now

and then he braces himself and waits: any moment now the tires will skid and everything will go out of control. The whole world, all of life, blurs into frenetic movement till the imminent crash seems, by comparison, pure mercy.

Fan mail, hate mail. Quotable and unquotable quotes. Questions, interviews, sweat and powder and flashbulbs. Bytes and more bytes, a world of biters and bitten.

Vested interests. Hinduization of the past. History as armor. History as propaganda. History as battleground. History as the seed of hatred. History in the hands of the mob. Conspiracy theories. Rightist conspiracies, leftist conspiracies. Foreign-handed conspiracies. A Babel of voices is trapped in Shiv's head, a play with a cast of thousands. These characters never stand still; they run from meeting to rally to interview. All of them have something urgent to say, and they say it in as many words as possible.

For instance: Guru Khote is addressing his third seminar of the week. He rounds off his talk with his usual trademark from the *Encyclopedia of Great Quotations*. He says with an air of supreme profundity, "As Thomas Paine said in *The Age of Reason*, 'My own mind is my own church . . .'" (Amita nudges Shiv. "You know what he is called in some circles, don't you? The Quote Guru.")

Professor Fraudley, the eminent Indologist no one had heard of till six months back, has flown down to Delhi to make his contribution via newspapers and websites. "As an international expert on all matters Indian, I have no hesitation in saying that Indian Culture has always been spiritual, and it must continue to keep its Spirituality Quotient (SQ) high."

Amar, committed young activist (CYA), distributes leaflets that scream in 24-point bold type: **Is the past up for grabs?**

Arya's hired students put up posters which reply, "Down with Foreign Craze! Long Live Patriotism!"

The erudite old historian Amir Qureishi is helped onto the stage to whisper passionately: "Identities are never permanent. This obsession with identity uses the past to legitimize the political requirements of the present."

The Manch spokesman froths at the mouth. "Who are these historians to talk when they don't know the first thing about the past? Man first took birth in Tibet, originally a part of Bharat. All beings were Arya beings. It is from there that they spread out into the fields. It is now 179 million, 19 hundred thousand, and 84 years since man stepped on this earth."

Guru Quote: "Who speaks for the people or their religious beliefs? As Swift said, we have just religion enough to make us hate, but not enough to make us love one another . . ."

Arya: "Are these foreign-lovers nationals of our land? We will accept only people whose loyalty to our traditions and our heroes down the centuries is undivided and unadulterated."

Fraudley: "Sanskrit is not a dead or elitist language. It is the symbol of cultural unity, and the ancient wisdom that helps us read horoscopes. Besides, computer scientists agree that Sanskrit is the ideal language for software."

Qureishi: "The nationalism practiced by these sullen, resentful, intolerant men is very different from the nationalism of the freedom struggle. This new brand of nationalism is monstrous. Look at examples all over the world."

Manch: "What can even a thousand policemen do when we emotionally charged people take to the streets?"

Amar: "The big picture is out of fashion. Now it is all specificities, a chaos of small pictures. Only caste, or only gender, or only environment. Next it will be a movement devoted just to the right to have an orgasm. All funding is for fragments of the big picture."

And Guru Q, coming up on stage to deliver "the vote of thanks": "If I may be allowed one last quote . . . h'mm—"

Arya: "They are all against Indian philosophy! We should not let them speak!" (The hired students kick aside chairs and rush to the stage and grab the mike.)

Ministers, lefties, righties, bandwagonwallas, touts, students, student leaders, spokesmen, spokeswomen. Rent-a-quote swamis, and their estranged cousins, rent-a-quote imams. Historians, journalists turned politicians, engineers turned linguists, computer experts turned archeologists.

In the middle of this dizzying circle, in the lone eye of the storm, Shiv waits with clammy hands and a weak heart. The beast is preparing to charge him, the beast with many heads, many masks, many voices. Is there no escape? Shiv could extend his leave, resign, then slip out of sight. His supporters, grateful as he is to them, unsettle him. The others, the fanatical revisionists, terrify him, bewilder him. What has happened to history, the history his uncle thought was a dull, safe choice of subject? It has become a live, fiery thing, as capable of explosion as a time bomb.

"It's got nothing to do with history, they're just goondas looking for publicity," says Amar's friend Manzar.

"I'm not sure it's so simple," says Amar. "This lot know how important it is to use the past in the present."

"I hate the thought of what their vigilance squad will find in the past next," says Meena.

"We can make a good guess," says Amar wryly. "They'll want caste and beef to do the vanishing trick, but we'll see Aryans sprouting all over the place."

"You mean the old made-in-India complex," interrupts Jyoti. "Next they'll be arresting anyone who doesn't think the first Aryans were born in India." She says to Shiv as if she has just made a discovery, "It's a battle for minds."

Shiv looks pleased and a little surprised that they should think alike. "Yes it is, isn't it?" Then he adds gloomily, "And perverting the collective memory may not help to write good history, but it helps to build national monuments."

"Forget all this endless going round and round," announces Meena. "The judgment is simple enough to fit into a few words. The Manch—your bloodthirsty munchies—will break and devour everything we have if we don't stop them."

Shiv's daily quota of love letters seems to prove Meena right. It's as if Arya has opened a tutorial agency for a whole army of letter-writers. Dear Sir, If the Muslims can have their fundamentalists, why can't we? Have we forgotten that Hindus have stood the test of time like no one else? Our fundamentalists have been around longer than theirs have. So we have to show the world we are superior to them in every way.

But there is, as always, the occasional lone voice or two. One for instance inquires plaintively, Dear Professor, What is all this needless noise? What does it have to do with Basava?

Less and less, as controversy's noisemaking machine drowns out the voices of Basava and his truth-telling river. Basava is no longer the cause though his name is bandied about by a few overnight experts. No one really remembers him—no one is struck by the stark, astonishing parallels between his time and the present—in the midst of argument and counterargument, threat and retaliation.

It is left to Shiv to play Basava's keeper. Though the lesson on Basava makes it to the papers and the television every other day, it seems to Shiv that he alone goes back to Basava as to an unmentionable secret.

What would Basava have done in his situation? Shiv has no answer to this absurd question he asks himself lying sleepless in bed late in the night. But the question does summon a series of fragmentary images, which when put together recall how fiercely Basava fought against the dissent-haters. Against his own version of the Manch and its cohorts. When did Basava first come face-to-face with *his* Manch? When did he see the temple's clay feet, decide that confrontation was the only option? "Look," Shiv wants Basava's ghost to tell him, "this is how it's done." But Basava is in the midst of the demanding crowds of his own world. It is for Shiv to seek the clues he so desperately needs, pick up those fabled lessons of history so that the same mistakes are not made again.

Going back to 1168, to an unsafe past that threatens to leak into the present, Shiv sees two images side by side, condemned to be coupled forever. There, to the left, is Basava confronting his Manch, standing up to what he passionately believes in; confidently leading his men and women through the intricacies of ideology and politics. To the right is the second image inexorably tailing the first. Basava's city Kalyana in the throes of descent into anarchy; into chaos that will mark the end of an era, of the city's brief season of greatness.

But the self (and the present) intrudes as always. In New Delhi, in his own city caught in a distinctly ignominious season, Shiv is in a meeting once again, though not the sort he has learnt to navigate in the Head's regimented, bureaucratic paradise. This is Meena's sort of meeting, attended by twenty "likeminded" people who seem to have spent most of their lives disagreeing with each other on their common beliefs. The meeting is held on neutral ground outside the university campus, in a grimy, characterless "conference room" rented by the hour.

The purpose of the meeting is to decide on another meeting. This sounds simple enough to a neophyte like Shiv, but apparently the first item on the agenda—whether they are to hold a public meeting or a rally—merits argument for a good twenty minutes. Finally it is decided that they will compromise and have both: a rally (but not a silent rally as one participant timidly suggests), followed by a public meeting outside the university gate.

Shiv would like to shed his accursed shyness (especially when words like discourse and rhetoric and *problematique* fly about him) and say, "Forget your little arguments, the enemy is almost at our heels! If this can happen to an ordinary, cautious man like me, what about you ideologywallas?" Luckily, no one seeks Shiv's opinion. It seems enough that he is there, a symbol, or a statue around which living, talking people gather to make plans.

They are seated in an untidy circle; unlike Shiv's university meetings, there is no pretense of tea, so they make do with glasses of cold water. Meena is not there; she has agreed to rest at home on condition that Shiv will tell her all about it, and that she will go to the "real" meeting that will follow. But Amar and a few of his friends are there today, sitting in a tightly knit group to one side; Shiv can practically see the red banner that holds them close together, an invisible label that screams ACTIVISTS! A few other "activists" are scattered across the room, mostly individuals who do not deign to join the bigger groups though they seem obsessed with them; their imaginary banners vary from pink to magenta. The rest of them are alleged intellectuals or merely "concerned citizens," wandering liberals in cautious search of temporary alliances.

One of the activists (a light pink type) now takes charge. He pulls out his mobile from his shirt pocket, glances at it, then switches it off with a flourish. He clears his throat. "About the public meeting," he says. "Let's decide who should speak so it doesn't get out of hand. Professor Murthy will say a few words of course—about five to seven minutes, Shiv?" (He nods in Shiv's direction, taking it for granted that he will agree.) "Other than Shiv, I think we should ask Guru Khote and Professor Qureishi to speak."

"Qureishi is in Italy," interrupts one of the intellectuals.

"I know," says Light Pink a little sharply. "His flight comes in tonight at twelve-thirty. He's having lunch with us tomorrow, Leena's going to cook lobsters. But I'll also call him first thing in the morning." He waves his mobile in the air as if to let them know his hot line is always open.

Everyone begins to speak at once. The list of names grows: an eminent Gandhian; an eminent lawyer; an eminent Indologist who trashed Professor Fraudley in a review last week; an eminent retired judge, still feisty though he is ninety-three and inclined to go off on a tangent. Objections to the names pile up with equal speed. Shiv begins to wonder if the public meeting will last all day and night if they have all the suggested speakers addressing the public.

Meena's friend Jyoti seizes her chance when there is a lull in the discussion. Jyoti has a small, finely chiseled face. But when she opens her mouth, any impression of delicacy is instantly dispelled by her piercing, emphatic voice. "I don't see why we should have only eminent people speaking," she says. "What about students? And women—from women's groups or just plain individual independent women? History has been a masculine exercise for far too long!"

An elderly citizen who has been quiet so far speaks up. "What about inviting a secular swami to speak? Swami Anand, for instance? After all, this is a broad front, and we have to make it as broad as possible." He is careful not to look at the activists' corner as he speaks, but they know all the same that what he is saying is directed at them. As if in response, Amar pulls his chair forward in a decisive way the Head would have envied. He holds several sheets of paper in his hand; all the heads in the room turn in his direction.

"I think we have a consensus here," he says suavely. "G.P. can begin with a few opening remarks." (G.P. alias Light Pink looks modestly at his mobile.) "Then we have Professor Murthy, followed by Professor Mookherjee, Mala Rao of the New Gandhi Foundation, Jyoti of the KNU students' union and Professor Qureishi. The rest of the speakers we can invite on the spot depending on who is there at the public meeting. Some of us will be on standby if we don't have enough speakers—though that is unlikely." (He pauses for the predictable chuckles; everyone stretches and relaxes, sensing the meeting is winding up and that the activists will do the needful.)

Amar says, "I have a list of things we need to get done—we have to be clear about who is doing what. There are the placards to be made—I think we have some left over from the last rally and we can recycle those. We also have a list of slogans you can add to. Then there are the leaflets to be printed, and we have to get police permission for the rally now that we have some idea of the route. And I have a petition I have drafted here with me—some of you have already made suggestions and I have incorporated most of these. All of us will have to collect signatures over the next forty-eight hours." Light Pink and some others reach out for their copies; Amar looks pointedly at the intellectuals but they seem absorbed in contemplation of their feet.

Meena sits in bed, the telephone by her, a long list of eminents in her hand. Shiv has provided her with the necessary nourishment for the endless phone calls she makes. Chocolate biscuits, a large packet of chips (mint masala flavor) and a one-liter bottle of Coke. She munches a biscuit and frowns at the crumb-covered petition lying on the bed. She sighs. "These eminents drive me up the wall," she says. She reaches morosely for the chips, hoping for some instant consolation. "I've called Eminent A to O and they all need coaxing and flattering one way or the other just to put their names to a simple petition. Not one of them offered to make a single call—they are too busy of course. Now I'm stuck with calling Eminent P to Z as well, and I especially loathe P. The first thing she'll ask is who else is signing the petition, just in case her name is sullied by lowly company."

"I'll call her," Shiv offers dutifully though P terrifies him with her voracious appetite for gossip.

Meena stops chewing and rewards him with a dazzling smile. "Tell her we'll put her name on top of the list," she advises. "She'll want to be in the papers." She returns to brooding over her list. "The trouble is that the battle lines are not clear," she mutters. "Look at all these alliances we have to make—" She shrugs at Shiv's silence, picks up the telephone again. Her spirits spring up with their usual elasticity. "I'll call Eminent Q then," she says. "He's an old bore and he'll want me to read out the petition word for word, but he's a good egg. I'll get him to bring his students to the rally."

Amar says to Meena, "I've brought you a good piece by Qureishi. He really tears apart all this nostalgia for the past, what he calls the essentialized past. He says it's just crude glorification of anything premodern and traditional."

Meena takes the essay from him, reads a couple of paragraphs quickly, then drops it on top of her stack of petitions, leaflets and pamphlets. "Did you hear about that twit Sharma's new critique of modernity?" she asks. "It seems he complained that when he was in Paris he had to go all the way to the countryside to see a cow. But when he got back to Mumbai, he could sit comfortably in the Sea Lounge at the Taj Hotel and look at all the cows he needs to see on the road."

Amar scratches his chin and stretches his legs out on Meena's bed. He looks as if he could do with a night's sleep. "So are the oilies giving you trouble?" Meena asks. (She turns to Shiv and grins. "That's the organization of independent leftists . . .")

"These broad-front squabbles are endless, and the pettiness of it all!" Amar says. "Now we have to learn to work with everyone from GROPE to PUKE. Next we'll have someone suggesting that Imam Asif should be part of our broad front!"

"So we can march with one gang of fundoos against another?" interrupts Meena indignantly.

But Amar is not yet done with his list of grievances. "And all this talk of how We are the same, We are one, etcetera, is just so much government-style talk. There's class, caste, religious community, gender, language—everything makes for difference. But have you noticed, whether it's the government or the cinema, everyone wants to tame this diversity. Pretend to play out a goody-goody scenario of Amar, Akbar and Anthony, three brothers who are variations of the same patriotic theme."

"Fine, we are all different," says Meena. "But can't we remain different and still have a language or two in common? Can't we have more than one voice or one identity?"

Shiv feels he is in a play, miscast as a protester marching down the road. How else did he get to be part of the march, not a mere onlooker or a victim of the traffic snarls around them? As they walk past the traffic stalled on the other side of the road, he sees a man in a jeep shaking his head in disgust as he slows down to a crawl. But most of the car drivers seem resigned to the delay, some craning their necks out of their windows to read the placards they are carrying. To Shiv's astonishment, a few actually snatch up the leaflets Amar's boys are distributing among bystanders and those waiting in cars, buses and scooters for the rally to pass.

It's the first time in his life that Shiv is expected to "raise" slogans. But there are so many voices, and such a variety of slogans being shouted simultaneously, that he can only make out a word here and there. Down, Down, he hears; or Shame! Then Zindabad! Followed, inevitably, by Murdabad! For a while Shiv tries mouthing the right catchword at the end of each slogan. Then Meena's friend Jyoti calls out in a spectacular, carrying voice, *"Hitler ki thi kisse yaari?"* The answer to this question—who were Hitler's friends?—comes back with an enthusiastic cheer from the marchers: *"Knickerdhaari, Knickerdhaari."* Shiv thinks of Arya's following of khaki-knicker bigots and he is overwhelmed by a great liberating urge to shout out loud. For a few minutes he actually yells himself hoarse; then he sees the university gate looming before them and the crowd already gathered there, and the words freeze on his tongue.

The public meeting. Shiv sees Meena sitting on the pavement nearby, her wildly painted cast stretched out stiffly, her crutch by her side. He moves toward her as to a magnet; but she is surrounded by a group of KNU students. He tries to catch her eye but she is talking nonstop, all her gestures expansive. Then Amar taps Shiv on the shoulder and leads him to the university gate, where television and newspaper cameras wait with their lenses ready to shoot.

When the flashbulbs stop, Shiv looks up, blinks, and takes it all in. There are almost as many policemen as there are protesters. Some of the policemen carry walkie-talkies; others carry lathis, and shields that look like they have been recycled from old cane chairs. Slowly Shiv begins to recognize faces in the crowd. Quote is there of course; and Qureishi, Italy-returned; and Light Pink is at the mike, holding on to it as if he has finally found his true love. All the usual suspects are there, the public that makes up most public meetings in Delhi. But there are also more new faces than Shiv had expected, busloads of students, mostly from Meena's KNU, and even some smart corporate-looking types. Then Shiv notices Menon and Amita at the back and is filled with inexplicable gratitude. They see him looking at them; Menon gives him an uncomfortable grimace, but Amita waves cheerfully. She whispers in Menon's ear; he shakes his head and continues to stand there, looking pained. Shiv sees Amita throw her cigarette to the ground, crush it with her shoe and make her way up to him.

"Can you believe the crowd?' she says to him in a low but excited whisper. "Menon's being absurd, he won't come up to the front because the cameras are here. He's afraid of being mistaken for one of the photo-op devotees." One of the corporate-looking couples Shiv had noticed earlier walk by.

"Who are those?" he whispers to Amita.

"Nobody I know," she says, looking them up and down. "Muppies, I guess."

"Muppies?"

"Shiv, where have you been? A muppie is a Marxist yuppie, of course—oh Shiv, look at that ridiculous man over there with the Clinton placard! What on earth does he mean?"

Shiv peers in the direction she is looking. There is a sea of placards before him and the names of the organizations are often longer than the slogans on the placards. Secular Women Against Patriarchy (SWAP); Forum Against Hindu Terrorism (FAHT); People's Association of Secular Scientists (PASS). The guiding principle seems to be the more the merrier, or the more diverse, the broader the front. Their slogans remind Shiv of the appeals to all possible gods that truck drivers paste on their lorries, not taking any chances; betting on all horses at one go. He sees placards saying everything from STOP TALIBANIZA-TION OF INDIA to HISTORY DESTROYED! to WHO'S AFRAID OF THE MANCH? Then he spots the placard Amita is talking about. A man with a ponytail, beard and thick glasses stands way at the back holding up a placard with a cryptic message. He is obviously so proud of it that he takes it to all rallies, whatever the cause. The placard says: CLINTON, GO HOME! DON'T DROP YOUR BALLS ON US!

The meeting proceeds more or less according to plan till Guru Khote takes the mike. The poor man is only on his fifth pithy quote of the day when a loud heckling voice calls from the crowd, "Pseudosecularists, Hai Hai!"

Other voices are raised, the crowd pushes and shoves as people try to shut him up.

Amar moves away from Khote and strides into the crowd purposefully, followed by two of his henchmen. As they pass Shiv, he hears one of them ask Amar, *"Usko medical kar do?"* Shiv has never heard the phrase "to make medical" before, and he can only imagine the young man means to make a medical case of the heckler. Shiv's heart skips a beat; his eyes search the crowd for Meena. But before the police realize something is going wrong, before Shiv can imagine a lathi charge or tear-gas shells into existence, Amar has reached the heckler and is persuading him to leave. All the while, he has a casual, restraining hand on the shoulder of his eager henchman.

Shiv and Meena watch the late-night news to see if the rally has been covered. Shiv sees himself on the screen, looking shifty and apologetic, saying his little piece. The news editors have reduced his seven minutes to an admirable ten-second sound bite; Shiv is impressed that even he can sound like a quotable politician. All the same it is so strange to see and hear himself that he misses the rest of the coverage in a jumble of swiftly passing images.

"Forty-five seconds," says Meena scornfully. "The government has even these glitzy private channels in its pocket." She jabs at the remote viciously and flips channels.

"Wait," says Shiv when he sees an interview in progress. "It's the VC!" KGU University's vice-chancellor, looking well-scrubbed and well-oiled, is holding forth on the official university reaction to what he mysteriously calls The Unfortunate Episode.

The interviewer is a pleasant young woman who is having trouble understanding the VC's mumbles, and his tendency to substitute *sh*'s for his *s*'s. It's obvious the woman has prepared for the interview but to no avail. The VC may hem and haw and mumble, and take a good five minutes to finish a simple sentence containing half a thought, but he is dogged. Whatever the question, however she puts it, he sticks like a leech to his one-point diagnosis.

"Sir, your University does not have students on campus since all your courses are distance education programs. There has been some speculation on where these students who vandalized Professor Murthy's room came from, and if they are students at all . . ."

She stops, flustered; the VC has turned away from her and is looking straight into the camera. "Shtringent action," he says, looking stern, "will be taken against those indulging in antisocial activities on campus." Then he thaws. "The real question is shecurity."

"Security? But sir, the identity of these intruders if that's what they are . . ."

"I was shaying, it's all a question of shecurity. We've shet up a committee."

The woman quickly interrupts, "A committee to examine the disputed lesson or identify the vandals or bring them to—"

"We have to undertake shecurity measures on a war footing. A war footing. The committee will discuss all necessary options."

"Options, sir?" The pleasant young woman is beginning to look a little desperate. "What are the options?"

The VC beams at her; this is obviously a matter close to his heart. Then he recalls he is on national television and that he is supposed to look grave at all times. He makes an effort to conceal his enjoyment and compose his face. But he is now relaxed, sure he is on home ground; confident, and by his standards, eloquent. "It's all the work of outshiders. There are some parts of the university walls that badly need repair—we are short of funds always. This is how outshiders get in and dishturb campus harmony. I have promised the university community that we will keep these outshiders out." (The VC cannot resist a momentary smirk.) "We will shtep up shecurity measures and see to their backshides."

The pleasant young woman looks resigned. She has decided it is best to stop pretending this is an interview; the sooner she lets him say his piece about university shecurity, the sooner they can both go home.

"First, the walls. Broken walls must be mended. We have to consider increasing the height of the walls, maybe even put broken pieces of glass on top. Interim measures can include barbed wire. We have already handed over shecurity to a reputed private company. They are expenshive of course, but I have personally pushed for a higher budget allocation for shecurity. This is a priority, after all. I have also asked the committee to shit down to talk about campus development. High on the agenda are walkie-talkies for shecurity pershonnel and better lighting at night. We have also shuggested to faculty members that they use good shtrong locks on all doors in the departments . . ."

Shiv carries a tray with Coke, a bottle of rum and a few glasses into Meena's room. "Oh thanks," Meena says. "You have to hear what Jyoti's got hold of—a vintage statement by the munchie historian A. A. Atre. It's heavy-duty, full of fundoo mumbo-jumbo."

Jyoti looks unenthusiastic, but Meena prods her. "Come on, Jyoti, be a sport." Shiv sits down by Meena's bed.

Jyoti stands in the middle of the room and hams for all she's worth, reading Atre's statement as if she is reciting a Sanskrit sloka in a querulous old man's voice. In the interests of authenticity, Meena supplies the sound effects—punctuating om's, um's and aha's at the end of every sentence.

"It is said: That is Fullness, this is Fullness, from Fullness comes Fullness." Full-l-l-ness. Jyoti holds the L till fullness swells, growing riper and rounder each time she says the word. "When Fullness is taken away from Fullness, Fullness remains. How many so-called modern thinkers understand this ancient premise of Fullness versus Void? Their shallow interpretations of our culture more than justify the brahmins' wisdom in keeping sacred texts away from the uninitiated. True Indians, whose souls vibrate to ancient truths, must reject modern errors and misinterpretations. Signed, A. A. Atre, history prof. (retd.)."

Meena hoots as if she has not heard Jyoti read the same thing before Shiv came into the room.

"You should be on the stage," Shiv says, laughing, but without the enthusiasm Jyoti's performance deserves. The trouble is that somewhere in the loyal recesses of memory, he can hear his own ancestors—nothing like Atre by any stretch of the imagination—intoning slokas with solemn devotion. Shiv drinks up what is left in his glass and gets up.

"This Aged Atre," says Meena, flaring her nostrils with contemptuous scorn. "He divides his time between ranting about the Great Indian Zero and the Great Brahmin Foolness."

But Jyoti is done with the comic possibilities of fullness. She says to Meena dolefully, "We can laugh at the kind of clowns they have now. But sooner or later they'll manage to acquire some reasonable fellows of their own."

"You mean the soft types and opportunists," says Meena, unimpressed.

"That's what I'd like to believe too, but—" and Jyoti adds with a confiding air that Shiv finds touching, "These communalists have screwed up our heads so badly that I think I'm getting paranoid. I'm also sick of being so fucking PC all the time. The next thing you know, I won't be able to wear a saffron-colored sari unless it has green stripes."

"Our paranoia is nothing compared to theirs," Meena consoles her. "During the 1993 riots in Mumbai, some people drove their cars onto Chowpatty Beach and shone their headlights into the sea. They were actually trying to ward off an imminent Iranian invasion."

Words, more words. But like everyone else—perhaps more than everyone else if he is to remain entangled with history—Shiv is condemned to wooing what Amar likes to call "the bigger picture." And the bigger picture, it appears, needs more words, more nitpicking. But which big picture will fit on this canvas that is getting smaller all the time? The world, that vast map of furrowed wisdom his father spread out for Shiv's delight, shrinks all the time in the wrong climate. An entire continent, or an ocean with its deep secrets waiting to be understood, is captured and tamed. Domesticated. Reduced to a manageable size. History, its layered terrain of past merging into present, shrinks to the size of a module, a black-and-white booklet of lessons. Then that too goes. There is only a lone, orphaned atom left behind, a sullen, impoverished particle of knowledge. The world and its multitudinous mysteries are reduced to precarious survival on a crude seesaw. saint versus leader, saint versus man. Golden Age versus Dark Ages. Hindu versus Muslim, Hindu versus Christian, anti-Hindu, pro-Hindu. Secularist, pseudosecularist, soft Hindu, rabid Hindu.

If there is only one way to know ideas or people or the past, why bother with knowing? Why not take Basava's suggestion, throw away the mind and the heart rusting from disuse?

Shiv's mind and heart are very much intact, but he still feels the fear of an endangered species whose natural habitat has been taken over. His savaged room: even its memory, the imagined memory of its ruin, suggests that all hope—of pretending it did not happen, that such a thing could not happen—is an illusion. Shiv's room in the university has been left in shambles, shards of glass and splinters of wood mingling with the remains of his books and files. The legacy of vandals. The spaces vandals have pillaged and violated lie across the vast stretches of history, doomed to desolation. And what difference now, in the ruins of memory, between Vijayanagar and his university room? Shiv's room, though a minor city, a city of mundane compromise, joins its grand, monumental ancestors. Perhaps it is only the padlock on his door that keeps out tourists in search of storytelling ruins.

NINE

OCTOBER 1–2

*A*ll day the telephone has been ringing for Meena. In between, she makes calls and passes on what she has heard. The night before, while they were being treated to the KGU VC's latest ideas on university shecurity, there has been what Meena calls a "crisis" in KNU. The details pile up with each call; who the characters are and what they did gets more colorful and lurid with each consecutive report.

After the first four calls, Meena tells Shiv, "It was just waiting to happen. Your Manch leader Anant Tripathi was at a boys' hostel on campus last night. Some of our people gathered outside to demonstrate—we can't let these fascist goondas spread their propaganda. But it was a peaceful dharna. Or at least it was till their goons went berserk and burnt a motorcycle parked outside the hostel. It seems they also hurt one of our students— they broke his arm."

After the eighth call, she says, "The trouble started soon

after the talk began. Some of their boys were making lewd remarks about our girls who were sitting outside the hostel shouting slogans. Our boys intervened and their lot went crazy. Of course they are now saying it's *secular* hooliganism."

After the tenth call, she says, "They're going to set up an enquiry committee. Do you want to bet it will be full of fundoos and wimps? The police have already picked up four of our students. They picked up two of theirs but let them off with a warning. Shiv, will you bring me all the newspapers? I want to read every single version."

Shiv feels he is in the middle of *Rashomon* or some such cleverly constructed film where the whole truth remains stubbornly elusive. Where even a semblance of truth can only be reached obliquely, by painfully piecing together fragments of stories told by different people of the same event. For instance:

The other side (or "they"): "Now that they have indulged in suppression of speech, the storm troopers of the secular fundamentalists, commies and women's rights activists are pretending to be innocent victims. These hypocrites pay lip service to freedom of expression but they gathered outside the hostel and tried to force their way inside."

Our side (also "our people"): "The pro-Manch boys teasing our girls are not even students of KNU. They came in with Tripathi and were inciting our students."

They: "Why should we spoil our own function? Some of the commie girls were deliberately dressed in provocative clothes when they sat there shouting obscene slogans. And it's not true that a student's arm was broken during Tripathi*ji*'s talk. This is sheer secular propaganda. That student broke his arm two weeks back in an accident."

Our people: "Even some of the bourgeois newspapers support our version. There was a reporter on campus last night and he saw one of their boys setting fire to the motorcycle."

By the evening, the Manch issues its press release: "We condemn the attempts of secular fundamentalists in KNU to prevent our respected leader Shri Anant Tripathi from engaging in a peaceful, informative discussion with the students. Their ideology of Hindu-bashing, authoritarianism and rumor-mongering now stands exposed."

Meena is gainfully employed, confabulating downstairs with Amar and his mass base to pin down a few viable slivers of slippery truth. Not one of them noticed when Shiv slipped out of the room.

Outside, the first light or two twinkle in the distant horizon. It is twilight, the hour in which things are not always what they seem. In this state of half-light, half-darkness, it is not difficult to believe that the garden holds an entire hoard of secrets, both dreams and fears.

Tentatively, almost with a fear of being caught in the act, Shiv recalls Rekha's words the day before.

Rekha does not know about Arya's heroics in the alleged faculty meeting, but she does know about Shiv's room being ransacked. She has called several times over the last few days, though most of these conversations have been easily swallowed up by the growing, interminable babble around Shiv. But one call was a little different. That was when he heard the momentary wobble of her voice before she regained self-control, so that he felt almost aghast: was that really the tough, smooth-talking Rekha he knew at the other end of the line?

"I do see you can't give in so easily," she said. "It's not as if I don't see the principle of the thing. But to be idealistic at such a time, and with such people!" Her voice shook again, then fell almost to a shamed whisper. "Don't forget, you're dealing with hoodlums who have pulled down mosques and churches that have stood for so many years. They've engineered riots, for god's sake, what's a little violence to them? And they're so powerful now. What can we do—Shiv, don't you understand? I'm afraid."

In the end it was Shiv who had to play the unfamiliar role of comforting her, protesting that she was imagining the worst. When he called her this morning, she was back to her usual self. Some instinct told him that he should pretend she had never revealed her clay feet. This was the only way he could protect her, not only from her moment of weakness, but also from her fear.

Now though, sitting alone, in the oncoming darkness colored by the day's remnants and a hesitant, milky moon, Shiv goes back to that one call. Finally, not much was said; but what was said (and left unsaid) has allowed him to see Rekha, and himself, stripped almost to the bone. A tongue feels compelled to explore the strange taste and feel of the cavity left by a fallen tooth. Shiv is that tongue now; he summons Rekha's words again and again, and the uncertain, almost pleading tone of her voice.

There is something poignant about her admission of fear. About the fact that she is as fearful as he, that they are both equals in vulnerability. That she is willing to share this knowledge with him. He feels oddly protective of this Rekha, who at least for the duration of a single phone call has admitted that she is not always forging ahead purposefully, as if she invariably walks in the sunlit blaze of day.

But still, his faith is shaken. Now there is no way he can tell Rekha her fears are well-placed; that among the anonymous calls he has been getting, there is one caller who knows he has a wife and daughter, and that they are in Seattle. That the caller, a man with an unnaturally gravelly voice, reminded him that no one was out of their reach, and especially not in America, where they have any number of "friends."

If Rekha too is vulnerable in more ways than one, how is he to negotiate the unknown world ahead? Call on his father, a mere ghost, to guide him, or Basava, a banned history lesson?

In the undergrowth behind him, a peacock cries plaintively, as if calling its mate to come home to roost. Shiv looks at the warm light in Meena's room that beckons him to a dubious safety. He gets up, goes into the house. But he bypasses Meena's room and makes his way upstairs to his desk. He must try once again to finish writing the new lesson on the medieval Vijayanagar empire. What else can a teacher do? What other weapons come to hand?

He forces himself to turn to the notes for the lesson that waits on his desk. But this is a lesson he has to write with some-one—many strangers, many hostile eyes—looking over his shoulder. He summons Basava's words for courage: *Cripple me, father, that I may not go here and there. Blind me, father, that I may not look at this and that. Deafen me, father, that I may not hear anything else.*

Shiv's own father, loving ghost, beams. His vapory face lights up with approval as it always does when Shiv forces struggling pen to paper.

But Shiv can also see the newspaper clippings of a near future, rows of bold letters that hang before his eyes like a thick curtain. He sees these letters form words, legible words. They

condemn—loudly—any image of the past that does not con-
form to current theology. He can hear, in the refuge of his
room, the watchdogs' interviews. "Professor Murthy has distorted historical fact. He has tainted the glory of the model
Hindu kingdom of Vijayanagar. He has underplayed the villainous Muslim sacking of Vijayanagar City."

Shiv turns away from the barking watchdogs. But now he
hears the plaintive, wheedling voice of the Head. "What are the
facts pertinent to the lesson? One: Vijayanagar was a glorious
Hindu empire, a peak, if you like, of the Hindu past and heritage. Two: the empire was defeated in battle and the great city
plundered by the Muslim kingdoms. Why not stick to these
simple facts?"

Despite Shiv's contempt for the Head, his stomach con-
tracts. Is it possible to write history—or anything else at all—if
you have to worry about your masters' objections, their venal
sentiments? Shiv puts down his pen and waits. Instead of his
notes, he consults his own memories of Hampi.

Vijayanagar, now a memory in rock and stone in the
Hampi ruins. Shiv visited Hampi in 1996, and despite having
read all the travelers' accounts available, he was unprepared for
the scale of the ruins. The stories of Vijayanagar that awaited
Shiv, the modern traveler in Hampi, were cast not only in
words but also in granite; their plot was a slippery, perpetual
engagement between history and myth. The exploits of deities,
legendary heroes and heroines, and their human counterparts
in history jostled for Shiv's attention in images painted,
sculpted and carved on stone. The overwhelming motif was
that of conquest. The recurring visual theme was the majestic
man-lion, Narasimha, like a fantastic incarnation of all the

qualities the kings who worshipped him wished for themselves; or the mythical Yali, a fearsome combination of a tiger, an elephant and a horse.

Hampi. Setting of the Hindu Vijayanagar empire in medieval India, designed to be a showpiece of Hindu might. A fortress capital city as the focal point of the empire, a city full of triumphal arches, aqueducts, thriving bazaars and trade, roads, palaces. Temples and more temples. Blocks of stone, rock, everything on a scale intended to dwarf and diminish the individual citizen. A city planned to flaunt its glory, intimidate the subjects into subjection. And all the grandeur, like its kindred great cities, invariably built on the blood and sweat of hovels swallowed up by time. Grandeur coupled with a single-minded quest for power, inextricable from images of violence. Behind the façade—the spectacle of the wonder-city, the palaces and poetry, the dancing girls dripping with jewels, the treasuries and temple-coffers overflowing with precious metals and stones— an age-old recurring motif of other, darker associations. Tribute, arrears, massacres with fire and sword, revenge, slaughter. Imperial glory, intimate with the landscape of the battlefield. Then fall, decay, and ruin.

That is the larger picture, the images and associations the historian on a field trip took in.

But Shiv also remembers: on his last evening in Hampi, he took an auto up a hill overlooking the river and the Vittala temple. The auto groaned its way up and spluttered to a halt. The driver, Suban, a namesake of one of the Deccan sultans, climbed the rocks with Shiv. Suban told Shiv about the loan he had taken to buy his auto, his three daughters between the ages of two and four, then pointed out a cluster of tiny stone gateways. Couples who want to conceive, Suban said, set up two vertical stones and a third on top like a roof. When the child is born, they return to remove the roof, leaving a miniature ruin.

Shiv sat with young Suban, looking at the spread of ruins before them. The sun had almost set behind the dark, brooding gopurams and boulders. Then Suban said, tentatively, "It must have been beautiful, they shouldn't have broken it down."

By "they" he meant Muslims, his ancestors, what he had now been given to understand as his "side." And he was offering Shiv an apology; Shiv was, in his eyes, a representative of the Hindu side. Shiv's name, and his knowledge of the stories he had told Suban about the Narasimha and Ganesha statues they saw earlier in the day, were enough to make Shiv a custodian of a mythicized Hindu past. A past reconstructed, complete with its glories and its suffering at the hands of foreign invaders, both equally evocative.

Suddenly, all of Shiv's reading and scholarly training, all his understanding of history as a social science, dissipated into the gathering darkness around them. He was naked, unprotected. He had forgotten who exactly he was; all the collective progress of the last fifty years had been torn off his body in an instant. It was as if recent Indian history, the recent history of his father's time and his own, never happened. As if Gandhi and Nehru and Ambedkar and Bose and all the other unnamed heroes of the recent past had never lived. As if they were, like some epic heroes, entirely products of an inspired collective imagination.

And Shiv's father: was that his lost, wandering ghost standing behind Suban and Shiv, his wordless sadness a question and a challenge? Shiv could hear him ask the questions that always haunted him: What kind of country poisons the minds of children, of its youth? And did we fight for freedom so we could divide this teeming, hungry house forever?

. . .

Shiv gets up, restless. It seems he is trapped one way or the other. If he goes down, he will have to enlist in the army Amar and Meena are organizing for battle. If he remains upstairs at his desk, he will have to write the lesson, separate the Hampi he saw in 1996 from the City of Vijayanagar it held more than four hundred years before.

He puts down his pen and stares out of the window. The moon has retreated behind a cloud. Now the night is dark and sulky, the kind that leaves stars entirely to the imagination. The sky hangs over the world with all its unfathomable emptiness, supremely indifferent to Shiv. He turns away from the window. How is he to write about Vijayanagar City—either its glory or its fall—as if it exists in a safe vacuum, as if Basava and his Hall, Shiv's university and its history department, do not intrude? He remembers how puzzled the young auto driver in Hampi was when Shiv tried to explain to him that they did not belong to two different sides. The driver, who had been friendly and chatty all day, withdrew into suspicious, uncomfortable silence after Shiv's attempted lesson. On the one hand, there is this teasing memory of the auto driver in Hampi, willing to bear an unnecessary burden of guilt, seeing himself as part of a battle in the past he knows nothing about. On the other, there is Shiv's own Manch, with their clamorous claims to Basava's legacy though they are ignorant of him and his times; though they stand for everything Basava fought against to his last breath. Shiv sighs. Is there a connection here he is missing?

Shiv would like to believe that it is Basava who links 1168 and 2000. Yet it seems it is not the dissident leader who is the critical link, but the hatemongers; the same manches that have sprouted in two times, centuries apart. Just as Shiv's history

manch has taken apart his world and challenged him to put
the pieces together again, Basava's manch set his city on fire.
Reprisal upon reprisal followed dissidence. Taxes were increased
to fatten temples. Merchants left in droves, unable to stand the
strikes, the insecure streets and the fresh taxes. And the movement: reprisals meant that all those who had learnt to shed
servility had to relearn it. Now even the washerman and the
barber and the prostitute had become dangerous enemies of the
state. Basava's men and women began deserting the city; those
who remained behind were on strike. Kalyana, hub of prof-
itable trade, heart of Basava's movement, was no longer recog-
nizable. It lay mauled, torn apart, its golden hours under cover
of darkness. The lamps were no longer lit as day passed into
night, but flames attacked the city's organs; smoke choked
them. Its moving limbs, the low-caste and untouchable hovels,
had caught fire.

And the Hall of Experience, Basava's great democratic
experiment that gave a voice to so many low-castes, women,
was never the same again. It no longer rang with voices in bliss
or voices raised in protest—a change that must have been
painful to Basava. And did he have an ominous surge of feeling
that the worst hour had only just begun?

What happened, then, to Basava's Hall? Though no history
book tells him what exactly happened to it, Shiv has, after all, a
few signposts for guidance: his own eloquent, recent examples
of vandalism. The mosques and churches desecrated or burnt or
broken down in the last decade; and closer in time, closer
home, his own little room at the university. Contemporary acts
of war. Surely these are part of the puzzle, surely they can help
him piece together what happened?

· · ·

But it is not till he is in bed, in the grip of febrile dreams, that Shiv finds a picture or two unfolding for his terror and edification. And it is not so much a picture that he can view as something separate from him, outside him, but a brief space of time into which he has slipped, a time when the curtain between past and present loses some of its opaque quality.

An image trickles through. Others follow. Shiv is in what appears to be a playground, a part of the campus he has never been to before. It can't possibly be night; but it is dark, or darkened, as if the sky has bungled its way into the midst of a solar eclipse. Shiv squints to try and get the skyline into focus.

How strange, he thinks, that building in the distance is so forlorn, like a proud orphan standing alone. It looks solid but empty. Its swollen old dome rides the back of the horizon, curves its spine into a gentle but distinct hump. Shiv stares unblinkingly at the building. He can almost see its loneliness float across, seep into his skin. It feels, this loneliness, like damp, unhappy mist.

But it's not mist; it's smoke. His eyes draw back from the horizon and the building. It's not dark either; and he's not alone. He can hear running footsteps. Someone pushes him aside, rushes ahead. Then more running feet. The feet grow arms, a head. In the head speaks a voice he knows. He turns around sharply, sees Arya.

Arya's face is bulbous, swollen with excitement. His skin shines with sweat. "Here, you'll need one of these," he says, and hands Shiv a pickaxe. Shiv takes it from him.

But what's it for? What does Arya want him to do?

"Wait for orders," Arya barks.

What orders?

"The signal, stupid," pants Arya, racing ahead like a blood-hound.

Now Shiv is closer to the building, though he only senses this. All he can make out is the tight circle of bodies like a well-fitting ring round the structure.

He stumbles, stops. He looks at the ground. What are these piles of ropes doing on the ground? And these iron rods and hammers and axes?

But when he looks up he sees that there is someone in charge of it all; the Head is here, and he knows what it's for. He's handing out supplies, one portion per hand, all fair and in order. The Head sees Shiv standing there, puzzled and uncertain, and he smiles charitably. "Do you know how easy it is to put oil and rag together, or flame and wood?" he asks Shiv. "How *easy* it is to make a stick of fire?"

Shiv drops his pickaxe and flees. He races ahead, in the direction Arya went, running headlong into the jumble of flashing yellow and orange clothes, flags, banners.

He is now in the belly of the crowd. An army so thick that he can no longer see. He can only hear and smell and feel, and how exaggerated, how cruelly vivid these heightened sensations are! From somewhere in the navel of the crowd, voices rise ceaselessly, exhorting the crowd to do their duty. The crowd roars, getting more restless every minute. It sways, one gigantic body with too many limbs. Shiv can smell the heat of this creature all around him, too close to him, sickly sweet sweat and incense robbing him of even the smoky, torch-lit air. But then a voice howls "Follow the front ranks!" And the crowd surges forward, screaming slogans, a roaring, hungry, single-minded sea.

Shiv claws his way out of the monster's belly, scratching,

biting, using his head like a battering ram, till he finds he is grabbing empty air. The crowd has left him behind; he can breathe now, though what he takes in, in large grateful mouthfuls, tastes stale.

He must look for Menon, he thinks. And there, like magic, Menon is lurking in the fringes as always. He must have Rekha with him. And Meena. Shiv stumbles forward.

But before he can get there, Shiv can see his father walking toward him. Shiv retreats. But the skeletal frame comes closer; now he can see the face, a skull's grimace within hissing distance: "Look!"

Shiv turns around, looks. Through the ghostly haze of fire and smoke he sees a dozen men brandishing rods and flags on the building roof. Then the dome comes down.

His head swings around, he looks indignantly into his father's prophetic face. But all he gets is a mocking, merciless taunt from the death-head: "How many more times?"

Shiv shudders, backs away, wakes up.

The light streaming in through the window is fresh, blissfully ignorant of troubled dreams. In the wholesome light of day, what went before is nothing more than a nightmare. Only a natural side effect of hobnobbing with the world's bloodthirsty munchies.

Shiv emerges from his room, strips, pours cold, purifying mugs of water on his head. He washes and scrubs, brushes and rinses, hawks phlegm and gloom into the bathroom sink till he feels himself again. The day waits ahead, with its glib promise that the night's fitful visions can be easily forgotten.

It was only a nightmare. But the nightmare has an undeniable aftertaste: a nagging fear that the night's ugly secrets will not stay within bounds. That if Shiv is not careful, the hatred he witnessed, the scenes of destruction, may leak into the day that waits downstairs for him. The unbridled chaos he left behind in sleep may catch up with him; demand that he return, relive it all once more. He has passed the night unharmed for the present. But who knows when it may come back again, play itself over in other places, other times?

TEN

OCTOBER 4–6

W hat does it matter one way or the other? It all happened long ago, didn't it? Only professors are obsessed with details. The rest of us only need to know enough to be proud of our past." His daughter Tara's message remains consistent to her principled indifference to making a fuss over principles. Rekha's most recent e-mail is equally short but more to the point: she has a confirmed ticket for October 28th, but she is also wait-listed for an earlier date. The brevity and matter-of-factness of her message remind Shiv that the rest of the world continues to go about its business; that normalcy is still alive. Its ability to survive will have to be his talisman against the dangers of the munchies' world—and perhaps Meena's as well.

But in the garden (Rekha's bamboo about Shiv) a howling fills the moonlit night. A jackal bays. A jackal whose cry seems to have sought out Rekha's garden, then broken into the wilderness of Shiv's heart, a scavenger's paradise.

In his study (the word now a misnomer), a conqueror of another sort, a conqueror of vandals, has been holding court. Meena has been in a peculiar mood since the broad-front rally to protest what she calls "the attack." There is something bubbling in her, a simmering brew of excitement, impatience, and to Shiv's surprise, a wariness.

He can sense her watchfulness all the time. He can sense that she is waiting for a critical moment. When he will break and she can swoop down, one-legged, one-crutched, to put the pieces together again. She seems to have summoned all the force at her command, concentrating it. Willing him to vault over some invisible trial of a hurdle to land on his feet, safe on the other side.

Sometimes he catches her staring at him as if her eyes can tell her what he is thinking. What he will do next. What he is worth. Once or twice he meets her look steadily. Their eyes hold each other in a no-man's-land of possibilities. Two pairs of eyes locked together, two walls leaning against each other, neither willing to give way and crumble.

For a moment Shiv pretends they are evenly matched.

Thursday morning. Kamla and her family have taken two days off to go to a wedding. Shiv and Meena are alone—or almost. There is the baby-faced security guard the university has recently employed to keep its historians alive. Meena has already made friends with him; he has told her that this is only his second assignment. He has also told her that if Shiv were a real VIP, there would have been two guards and he would have had company. As it is he keeps boredom at bay by standing outside Meena's window and watching television through the torn mosquito screen. He prefers film song-and-dance shows; his secret desire (which Meena of course knows) is to make it as a hero, or at least a villain, in a Bollywood movie.

For the moment Babyface is in his makeshift tent on the front lawn, pottering around, performing domestic chores without self-consciousness. He seems to think Rekha's garden has grown walls that protect him from the public eye. His gun—which Shiv would like to believe is unloaded, merely a potent symbol—lies casually on the grass, a clump of beedi and cigarette stubs nearby.

Meena is bathed and radiant; the plump black snake of her hair glistens with water. She sits in bed, propped up against fresh pillowcases, newspaper open at the edit page. Shiv can see a cluster of beads that her towel has missed, little globules of moisture on the curve of her neck. Every time her head moves, the swollen beads tremble. Shiv's fingertips covet their glitter. Their diaphanous spots of skin.

"Shiv!" she exclaims, her head jerking up with excitement. The beads shiver, then trickle down her neck. "There's an edit about the attack!" The beads are gone but her eyes have inherited their sparkle.

"Listen," says Shiv's young mentor, an unlikely reincarnation of his father.

Shiv makes himself look away from her neck, her eyes. He forces his attention back to her words as she reads aloud.

"It's called 'Whither History?'" she announces, rolling her eyes to tell him what she thinks of the title. "But the edit's not bad at all."

"There are several lessons to be learnt from the recent ransacking of a professor's room in K.G. Central University in Delhi."

(Meena's lush eyebrows rise in appreciation.)

"About thirty young men claiming to be students took the University authorities by surprise when they stormed into the History Department on the twenty-fifth of this month. The incident has been 'explained' by the Itihas Suraksha Manch as 'a spontaneous protest by students against the distortion of heroic historical figures and the anti-Hindu bias' of a lesson on medieval history written by the professor in question."

("I don't know why they're so coy about mentioning your name," grumbles Meena.)

"What makes this an ominous development is that there seems to be tacit sanction from the powers that be for any lunatic fringe that does its dirty work."

("Not bad, huh," asks Meena, looking cheerful again. "Raj Choudhry must have written the edit— something to be said for these old-fogy liberals." Then she remembers she is talking to a similarly afflicted audience, and quickly returns to the edit.)

"Even despots have fought shy of openly declaring they are rewriting history. But what used to be secretive has become respectable government policy, with textbooks being 'rewritten' to give them a certain slant."

("H'mm, he could have spelt it out, don't you think? Watch out, I think he is about to speechify now.")

"All this has to be viewed as part of a larger process to deny the composite nature of Indian culture. We have been witness to several crude attempts to go back in time, hundreds of years, to deny that non-Hindu traditions, or 'little' traditions that are critical of the mainstream tradition, have also contributed to the country's social, cultural and political life. We seem condemned to endless replays of the demolition mindset. The Babri Masjid was first marked as a 'disputed structure,' then demolished 'to set right historical wrong.' This time round, what is being marked as disputed territory, what is being assaulted with a view to demolition, is not just academic freedom."

(Eyes shining, a fleck of saliva glinting at the corner of her mouth, Meena mouths the blaring of trumpets—ta-da-daah!— before she reads the next sentence with the emphasis befitting a climax.)

"It is the right of a people to a complex, pluralistic history. It is true that history is not an indisputable body of knowledge. But history itself shows us that attempts to 'rectify' it have all too often been camouflage for the doctoring of history."

Meena races through the last couple of sentences; too obvious, she says, to be interesting. Then she tosses the paper to Shiv, gloating. "See? There are all kinds of people on our side."

Shiv notes the *our* in place of *your*. He tries to smile in appreciation as he takes the paper from her. But he feels his stomach muscles tighten by reflex as if Meena—and the absent Amar—are appraising his fitness.

Later, alone in bed, the projector in Shiv's head plays its latest home movie to a captive audience of one. Several screens flicker to life simultaneously. In the screen at the very center, Meena fills the frame for an instant. Then her full, generous body shifts to make room for Amar. They sit on the same bed; his foot rests close to her cast. Shiv can see Amar's toes, their nails overgrown and dirty, brushing the plaster on her thigh. She holds out her half-eaten bowl of ice cream; Amar helps himself to a spoonful. They finish the bowl together, both using the same spoon. Amar leans forward to take the draft she has prepared of the new leaflet. His hand moves toward hers. His arm—is that her breast it grazes so casually?

The mind is the snake; the body is the basket. They live together, the snake and the basket. You don't know, though, when it may kill you; you don't know when it will bite! Shiv turns to the other side, impatient with himself. Impatient and sick at heart.

Meena is still there on the screen, but Amar has moved out of the frame. Now it is Babli who runs in, excited, calling Meena Didi to come look at what she has found outside. She hands Meena her crutch and hurries her out of the room. Just outside the front door of the house, Rekha's jasmine plants bristle with swollen green caterpillars. Babli picks up one with a stick and throws it to the ground. It wriggles in protest, then crawls back to the plants. Babli stamps on it; the squashed caterpillar leaves a gray sticky mess on the ground. Meena calls from the door, "Wait, that will take too long. We have to do it properly. Go to the kitchen and get some matches, then help me out of the house."

Babli has left with the last of the caterpillars. Meena is back in her room; it is late in the night. Meena takes a bottle of water to her mouth. Shiv can see her throat stretched back in an arc as she drinks. As always she drinks too fast; some of the water spills on her chin, trickles down and wets her neck and T-shirt. She puts the bottle down, yawns, blinks. She reaches under the pillows, pulls out one of the booklets she has earlier persuaded Shiv to read. *The Politics of Hate* perhaps. *Onward United Action.* Or *Women's Voices and the Communalist Agenda.* Meena reads a few pages, yawns again. She drops the booklet on the floor, reaches once more under the pillow and finds Shiv's indulgent tribute, *Asterix and the Normans.* She settles down on the pillows to read about Justforkix who needs to be made a man of, and the fierce Normans who don't know the meaning of fear but are hoping to find out. Meena's eyes close; the comic slips out of her hands, falls to the floor.

Meena, at the very heart of things. But there are also the other screens on display tonight, not to be wished away because they are in the background. Shiv ignores the images of crowd scenes; he pauses at the frame that holds hungry Amita, groping at anything that will help her lose herself in a moment of excitement. Shiv sees the hope on her face; once more she is pretending she need never return home again. Shiv moves away, edges his way gingerly past the screen with two larger-than-life silhouettes, the whispering, discontented ghosts of his father and Basava. *(Like a monkey on a tree it leaps from branch to branch: how can I believe or trust this burning thing, this heart?)*

And then, as always, the frame that will always be there, the frame that holds Rekha. Competent, thorough Rekha, an expert at keeping up appearances. Shiv sees Rekha, arched eyebrows raised as if she is assessing something, her sari and hair held firmly in place with an assortment of pins. (Shiv has for the moment forgotten, or misplaced, his glimpse of a frightened, vulnerable Rekha.) It has been years since Shiv had an inkling of what she feels about him. Rekha, poised wife at all times, knows just when to move, when to go limp and lie still. But the face he sees before him does not look like it belongs to the overseer of a well-oiled machine. Her face now has a look of pensive waiting, as if she has many more years to go before she is let out on parole for good behavior. Shiv tries to remember where he has seen this look before. Then he places it: it is the look of someone, a tourist perhaps, who has overstayed in a small, boring place. She has nothing left to discover, but there are weeks of emptiness stretching before her, empty days and nights she must will herself to fill. Rekha's face says she has seen everything there is to see; she has seen through Shiv. Having exhausted emotion, all that remains is habit. The management of the masks she presents to the world; the management of his small, drifting life.

Shiv squeezes his eyes shut, desperately trying to fall asleep. But a little question or two lie in wait on the road to oblivion. What does he look like in their private nightly screens, in Amita's, Rekha's and Meena's? If Meena could see the moving images in his head, she would ask this question sharply, defying him to answer. Where does he fit in the place where neither censor nor peeping Tom can follow?

Friday evening. Another setting sun, an overripe orange hanging low in the sky. Shiv sits by Meena; close to her bed. Sitting close, one track of awareness on the conversation. The other track, the hungry, grasping one, looking. Looking at an arm: Shiv's eyes move down Meena's sleeve, then down an inch of skin followed by an elbow with a gray dry patch. Another two inches, past two small abrasions, one red from scratching, the other scabbed. Then the forearm with its fine dark down, soft and untouched. The hand. It moves carelessly to the scab, picks at it experimentally, loses interest. A hand that does not know what other hands would give to go where it goes so casually.

Hands. A tongue. Why have these if she cannot know them?

The guard's radio comes on with a burst of static, then thankfully gives up the ghost. Shiv draws the window curtain and returns to the chair by Meena's bed.

What should he talk about? How should he pretend he is here to talk? But he must. He must begin a conversation, keep it going, so there is no question of having to leave the room. If he talks, a gift may come his way. A quickening of response in the eyes, or a smile, or even a full-fledged laugh with its flash of even white teeth. But he doesn't know where to begin. The Decision, or What I Will Do Next, lies sullen and heavy between them, a better watchdog than the gun-toting man in the tent.

Meena too remains silent. There is no use pretending she cannot read his mind, or that she has not diagnosed at least one of his sicknesses. She has read the doubts that lie like an inch-thick layer of dust on Principle and Strength of Purpose. She has seen his fear that he will not be able to sustain his quasi-heroic stance for much longer.

Shiv forces himself to look into her face, a masochist preparing for her scorn. Her disappointment. He steels himself to meet the look that will tell him he will fail.

But what he sees on her still, attentive face is more than the now-familiar watchfulness. There is also something new, the glimmer of something hard and flinty in her eyes. A determination, as if the way out has just been revealed to her. As if she has, in anticipation of his dithering, made some irrevocable decision on his behalf.

Words, those tenuous links that chain them together syllable by syllable, have at last failed them. The silence between them stretches into a long, unbearable intermission. Life before this pause is over and done with. But when will the afterlife begin? And how do they get to it?

They watch each other, one waiting for the other's move. Waiting to see which of them will dare to come out into the open, declare predatory intentions.

Shiv tells himself: It is important never to hurry. The beloved object is in sight. I know my destination; I know it only too well. But I must pretend (just a little longer) that it is obscure, that I am not even aware of it. I must ignore my heartbeat, the insistent throb of my pulse. The inevitability of inhaling and exhaling. Breathing is more natural when you are not conscious of it. It doesn't stop or go away just because you are not looking at it.

Meena too is still: a clear, waiting sky, looking on unblinkingly. Shiv is the cloud. All the desire in the room—and there is so much of it, the air is thick with humidity—is concentrated in him. She must know how he feels—or she must know something of it. She must see, even she must see that he is on the brink of more than one precipice. Sense his ache for her, forever coupled in his mind with the fear of living with danger, choice, commitment. Fear of his new life, a small room crowded with strangers. With thugs, bare knives glinting in the dark. He must take hold of it all, claim his life as his own.

Shiv gets up, pushes his chair back. He picks up the sheet she has tossed aside. He folds it carefully, places it on the table. Then he finds himself approaching the bed in a smooth, continuous movement as if the chair has dissolved once he has left its refuge.

His feet slip out of his rubber chappals; he sits on the edge of the bed. He takes a hand, one of her hands, in his.

She suddenly jerks free, struggles to a sitting position, and slaps her unbroken knee. She lifts her skirt, picks up the corpse of a mosquito between her fingers, her face gloating; she crushes it though it is already dead. Then she lies back, restores her hand to his. Her fingertips feel sticky.

She looks so matter-of-fact. So removed. But she does not resist. Instead, despite her casual, noncommittal air, she reaches over and her free hand strokes his arm gently. As if to give it courage. Take it forward. His mouth dries; it is hard to breathe. A charge, a low-voltage current, passes through his stomach then travels downward.

The guard's radio sings aloud for a minute, dies again. Then there is a thud; he seems to have given up on the temperamental thing and flung it across the garden.

Shiv takes the hand on his arm and guides it down his belly. But Meena takes it back and places it chastely on his shoulder. He pauses, afraid he has misread her touch. He steals a look at her face. Her eyes meet his steadily. There is no invitation there, but it is clear, even to him in his confused and excitable state, that she is saying: Decide. Enough dithering. This is the signal picked up by his eyes, hands, lips, and tongue, all at the same instant.

The lightbulb in the room surges, dims, surges again. Then the power goes. A hush settles on the room without the droning hum of the fan and cooler. The room turns dark and stuffy.

Shiv kneels precariously by her good leg, bends over her, lips and hands skimming lightly over bare skin first: her face, neck, arms. His hands feel damp. Meena's forehead tastes of salt.

He sits back on his haunches and slips a hand under her T-shirt. He rolls it up gently; she is not wearing a bra. He gazes worshipfully at the shadowy mounds of her breasts. Then he lays a finger, and a thumb, on one brown nipple.

He looks at her face again. He squints in the gathering darkness, trying to read her expression. He thinks he sees her lips part; he waits to hear her moan. Instead he hears a singsong buzz that begins somewhere behind him, then darts across the room and back. Silence for a moment; then Meena brushes a breast indignantly and the fly takes off, lands on his neck.

He hears a gentle, exhaling hiss from Meena, but he can't decipher it. Then silence again, a dense, weighted silence. The bed, the room, float free in time and space. His thighs hurt.

The fan and cooler return to life and fill up the room with their background music. But it remains dark; the lightbulb must have fused when the voltage went berserk earlier.

Shiv gets off his haunches and takes the measure of Meena's cast. He balances himself carefully, one kneeling knee on either side of her wide hips. His torso hovers over hers. He bends over a breast; his lips meet a taut, hard nipple. His hand stretches down, explores the hemline of her soft skirt.

The doorbell rings; Shiv ignores it. His hand is inching its way up her good thigh. Someone taps loudly on the window, then they hear the baby-faced guard call.

"What is it," Shiv says dreamily, his hand now between her legs—or between a leg and a cast.

"My radio is not working," Babyface informs him. "And there are a lot of mosquitoes here." Shiv can see Meena's grin clearly in the darkness. He removes his hand from under her skirt and takes it to her lips, traces the outline of her smile.

Babyface is not discouraged by Shiv's silence. "It's time for *Boogie-Woogie*, sahib," he now says. "I watch it everyday. Can I come in and switch on the TV? The power's back."

Meena shakes with laughter as she pulls down her T-shirt and pats her skirt into place. "Let him in," she whispers to Shiv. "Don't be a spoilsport. We'll watch it too and give Babyface some tips for his Bollywood career."

Meena, at the very heart of things. Meena, a sweet and disturbing mixture of irony and inexperience. Meena, whom he has just about touched; who transformed him, for all of fifteen minutes, to a simple organism that is all (and only) hands, lips, tongue.

And afterwards, despite *The Boogie-Woogie Show* and Baby-face, despite the return of his mind and its chaotic jumble, the astonishing sense of oneness. Shiv feels—and even young Meena cannot take this away from him—that they are as close as they will ever be, regardless of what was done and not done. It is surprising how little the details matter. He has the sense that they have given each other something that is, for all its namelessness, more solid and memorable than actual physical love. And this, regardless of the promise she has extracted from him, though they did not exchange a word about it all evening. Oh yes, he is not entirely deranged by middle-aged lust. Even when his hand first touched hers, he knew there would be a price to be paid, a price only she could help him pay. A promise to stand firm, to resist giving up. A promise bigger than both of them; a promise he has made though it may change his life.

But what she has drawn out of Shiv without the crutch of words does not come between them. It leaves untouched the bit of land they own together. There is no law, no government, no ghost that can tell them how they should cultivate it, when they should let it remain fallow. With Meena at the heart of things, all backgrounds dissolve, then re-emerge with one coherent image of union. A center filling up the frame. Though his shadow sniggers a little, Shiv recalls Basava's poem on the one-ness possible between a man and a woman: if a man and a woman really look at each other, a union is born; a union fit to unite with the lord of the meeting rivers.

ELEVEN

OCTOBER 10–13

Saturday, Sunday, Monday; three whole days since Friday evening. Though Shiv and Meena have not so much as touched each other since, though Kamla is back as chaperone and keeper of propriety, he still feels a steady surge of newborn hope. He still feels blessed. He could swear he is ten pounds lighter.

Not long ago (twelve days? fifteen days?) his room at the university was stripped bare and a new padlock put on the door. A lock to which he does not have the key. But he is in such a state of grace that he finds himself entertaining a few grandiose thoughts. Could he have tired of a lifetime in one night? A lifetime of spineless liberty from commitment?

Meena's searching eyes follow his every thought like a flashlight, but she too appears calm. Quieter, less excitable than usual. (Perhaps she is not entirely untouched by what he feels for her?) Even when the doctor looks approvingly at a fresh

X ray and tells her that the hated cast will come off in a matter of days, her joy is muted. They seem to have declared a moratorium on all unrestrained emotion. On anything that may get out of hand and upset the delicate balance between them.

Maybe he is imagining the change in Meena. But is there a little uncertainty in her now, a cloud to disturb her clear, sectarian sky? Are there more dimensions in her world, more unknown spaces and gaps?

In keeping with this lull, this sleepy-sweet interval following the intensity of the past few weeks, the "case" too is on hold. After the vandals' orgy of destruction in Shiv's room, and the ensuing noise of charges and countercharges, support and condemnation, a curtain of silence has fallen on all stages. All fronts. As if the players concerned have agreed, even the most bitterly contesting ones, to retire backstage and recoup before returning to the fray.

The phone has not rung once for Shiv. The papers, the TV, the University, the Manch, Amar's band of saviors—all seem to have forgotten the notorious professor, along with the glories of Kalyana's temples and the truth about Basava's life and death. Both supporters and opponents have either been stunned into silence, or satiated by the most recent act of violence. And the public? They have now been pushed onto a moving conveyor belt of stories-in-transit. Two news stories far more engaging than Shiv's have been hogging the limelight for the past three days.

The first is a "high-profile" hit-and-run incident involving six affluent college boys. They apparently decided, at four in the morning, on their way home from a party, to test-drive one of their parents' Mercedes. Whether the car lived up to its manufacturers' promises is not known. What the car (or its driver, or its occupants) did manage to do was mow down a family of pavement sleepers. A night watchman nearby and a milkman on his early morning rounds are eyewitnesses. The night watchman identified the car's license plate; he and the milkman have described what happened.

The car flew down the wide and empty road, screeched around the roundabout and turned onto Ring Road, climbing the pavement and running over four sleeping bodies before the driver could bring it to a halt. Three of the boys are management students, two of them final-year law students. The driver has just got his American visa. He has, plead his parents through his lawyers, a promising future in information technology.

There is the usual spate of "man on the street" interviews. The usual moral indignation about what the youth are coming to. (Or where they are going to.) A couple of professional letters-to-the-editor writers rave about the damage foreign cars are wreaking on Indian roads and morals. There is also the smaller group of the usual suspects, mostly lawyers and relatives of the accused, spinning out tearjerkers about the heartbreakingly bright future stretching before these dazzlingly bright boys.

The incident recalls to Shiv's mind his encounter with the Mitsubishi boys on the day he bought Meena's crutches. Mitsubishi, Mercedes, the brand name is immaterial. The car in question is usually expensive, foreign, big—certainly bigger than his, a shamelessly middle-class Maruti. More important, its occupants are thugs at large. How can he forget his Lancer thugs? The thugs who thought themselves heroes? He can never forget the identical masks on their faces. Masks frozen in his memory, with their potent combination of threat, derision, amusement. Their confidence that they will prevail, that no man or law can touch them. Their simmering energy, their unbridled aggression, their lethal boredom.

But as a story in transit, a story to distract Shiv from the real plot unfolding about him, the Lancer boys' misadventure is not a success. Their threatening presence is far too close to his bones; they do not appeal to his sense of the ridiculous. How do you make the question *What is a man?* funny, at least for men?

It's the second news story that provides Shiv the comic relief he craves. Most of the story is pure froth (and skin), though it generates a pro-and-con discussion as passionate as that provoked by the Lancer boys.

Miss India, a lissome twenty-two-year-old called Nixie, has just returned to Delhi as Miss Universe. (Nixie explains that her father visited the US for the first time when Nixon was president.) Indian Beauty Rules the Universe, gushes a headline, but young Nixie is not satisfied. She holds a crowded press conference, wearing her royal white gloves and fake diamond tiara. Everything else, she explains proudly, is homegrown. Her strappy sequined dress, her hair, nails and teeth are all examples of Indian couture by Indian designers, specially created for the occasion.

Nixie gets a little tearful when asked about the party-poopers who have been saying nasty things about beauty contests. "I think they are very negative," she says firmly. "There is such a thing as Beauty with Purpose."

In fact, says Nixie, she has returned to Delhi with a promise. She is going to spend the rest of her life working in Mother Teresa's mission houses. But obviously she has to complete her year's reign as Miss Universe first.

An unfeeling reporter asks her a pointed question about how this year as "queen" will advance her plans for the rest of her life.

"This year is going to be important training for my charitable work," Nixie says. "It will give me the experience I need in interacting with all sorts of human beings."

The silly season promises to continue all week. Thursday, Nixie and the Lancer boys compete for media space with a new story, Meena's favorite among the recent crop. Two magicians have been issuing challenges to each other via the press. One of them, a venerable old magician, has made the Taj Mahal disappear for forty-five seconds in the presence of journalists. His challenger, a young upstart who calls himself I. M. Jaduwala, claims the Taj trick is nothing: *he* can make Parliament House disappear for sixty seconds, even when Parliament is in session. What he promises is an out-of-body experience for the Indian state for all of sixty seconds. An entire headless minute.

"If I have made even women disappear," he boasts, "why should this be difficult?"

Meena is charmed by I. M. Jaduwala and his promise of a one-minute vanishing act. But as even Jaduwala will admit, magic is not permanent. Even as Meena and Shiv enjoy Jaduwala's pranks, Shiv's minute-long reprieve is drawing to its inevitable end. The university and its controversy—though Shiv had dispatched both to temporary oblivion with a dubious magic—is even now on his way back to him through a special delivery letter.

Though he and Meena have not spoken of it, Shiv has heard, over the last few days' interregnum of peace, the countdown.

The alarm clock muffled by the pillow, still ticking on. The promise has been floating between them, alive though it is only an embryo. Soon the choice will have to be made in real life, a choice that cannot be undone so easily; in words that cannot be taken back. The ticking can no longer be ignored.

The doorbell rings.

Babli, who runs to get it, returns with a letter.

The envelope, a brown official missive delivered by a university messenger and sanctified by the university logo, is addressed to Shiv, not from the Head, not from his boss the Dean, but from the university's shecurity-loving vice-chancellor.

The letter is couched in the kind of officialese that pretends its contents have no mortal sender or receiver. All it recognizes is the voice of a god. Or the voice of a hollow god, coming out of a megaphone suspended midway between heaven and earth.

This impersonal, unfathomable voice informs Shiv that "the recent incident with relation to our course material in medieval history has been most unfortunate." It wags a stern if invisible finger and goes on: "This is the sort of thing that brings the university disrepute."

The sermon ends with a constructive suggestion, taking its cue from a B-grade Hindi film attempting patriotism with an eye on a tax-free certificate. "Everything we write and teach should illustrate, without leaving room for doubt or ambiguity, that we are one country. Above all, nothing we say or write should have divisive consequences."

It is like looking at an image where the photographer has made a deliberate choice of depth of field. History in the foreground—what happened recently in Shiv's university room, for example—is entirely out of focus. The letter does not contain a single word about what the "unfortunate incident" is. The ransacking of Shiv's room is clearly a footnote, a minor by-product of "divisive consequences." What really matters—the unfortunate incident sharply in focus in the background—is still the original sin. That his lesson, his words, invited an unwelcome spotlight, the lurid colors of scandal and controversy and "politics" into the university.

"I wonder who wrote it for him," Shiv says to Meena. "I wouldn't have thought any of his ghostwriters knew the word *ambiguity.* It must have been the Head. Or the Dean, in spite of all his liberal-ethnic office décor."

But for once Meena is not interested in trashing a piece of official communication. "The real question," she says to him, "will come soon, but not on record. Not in writing. Maybe the telephone will ring. Maybe it will be face-to-face. Shiv—whatever the pressure, whatever the means of coercion—" She pauses.

Her doe-eyes turn shrewd and canny. Then she proceeds to a swift, neat attack. "Are you going to stop talking to the media? Extend your leave? Resign?"

Shiv stands before the bathroom mirror, shaving.

There is a lighthearted butterfly in his stomach, fluttering with tense excitement. There are many hours left for his visit to the university in the company of his bored bodyguard. But he feels, as he did all those years as a student facing exam day, that he must get every detail right. Perform every ritual that will guarantee the magical appearance of the right words, however difficult the questions lying in wait.

He spreads the foam carefully with the brush. Then as he turns to pick up the razor, his eyes catch sight of the sky hanging outside the window. Though it is still summer in Delhi, the sky looks dour and anemic. The sun should be blazing, but it is playing truant.

There is something familiar about the sight, the grayness leaking into light and blotting it out.

Shiv turns back to the mirror and takes the razor to his cheek. Once he has finished, he examines the results closely. On impulse, he pats his graying mustache with the foam and shaves it off. The bare face that emerges looks astonishingly like his father's last photographs.

His father. What happened to him, where did he go?

Shiv picks at these questions, familiar scabs that have grown back though he has peeled them off a thousand times before.

He has an entire catalogue of scenarios in his head, indexed, ready to be pulled out and considered, over and over again. Speculative summaries of the past, written in a script that is now lost to human knowledge.

Sometimes Shiv thinks it must have been a peculiar progressive sort of amnesia. His father loses his memory; bit by bit first, then chunks at a time. Maybe he consults a doctor. Maybe the doctor tells him to go to a psychiatrist, or tells him it's nothing, he is imagining things. Maybe the doctor has a diagnosis, a hard, cold name for it all. An -itis or an -isis that can never be escaped. His father decides to make his own arrangements. The details are immaterial; what is important is that if his past is to be moth-eaten, filled with enlarging holes, it might as well be taken away from him immediately. He might as well go forward (or backward) to meet it; become part of it; become the past.

That's the heroic scenario.

In the other, the more poignant script, the central image is that of his father, back bent. Here he is not suffering from a loss of memory. The diagnosis is a loss of heart. The country he fought for has turned its back on him. The world he knew has gone, left him behind. Why linger if his voice is unheard? If he is such a dinosaur, he may as well be one of his fellow freedom fighters, their lives extinct, their dreams congealed in stone statues, mute receptacles for bird droppings.

Nehru, the symbol of independent India his father believed so passionately in, is losing his aura. It's no longer 1947, glory glimmering in the midst of the ruins of partition, hope raising its tired head though it lies on soiled, bloody ground. It's 1962. The sheen of nationalistic fervor is long gone. The fabric of the new republic is fraying rapidly. Even the relatively privileged, those who have the luxury of acquaintance with concepts of freedom and independence, can see this.

Or Shiv could put all these imaginary cards back into the cupboard, reject their hieroglyphics as so much indecipherable nonsense.

In the only scenario left, the story is a particularly banal one. The man does not choose to disappear. He has no control over his fate; he does not lift a finger. He is a mere victim, a statistic. He is there, fragile, vulnerable, inviting disaster. He is shuffling along the platform, maddeningly slow. The train is to halt for five minutes. He is looking for water to fill up in his bottle or something to read for the rest of the journey. Or he has wandered off the platform, looking for a stretch of field by the track cleaner than the train toilet.

Then, obliterating past and future, severing the connection between them forever, a fist meets his chin; or a knife his back. Or a dirty rag is thrown round his throat and tightened. A commonplace robbery, a commonplace murder. All it takes, finally, is a few minutes, just a few minutes when the world goes crazy, for a freedom fighter to fall.

The stain spreads, the gray deepens. The sky turns a shade darker. The storm Shiv's life has been caught in for the past few weeks has tired of buffeting him about. It has now moved on. It has found a worthy opponent in the sky, the trees, all of nature, bent on survival despite the costs.

Shiv goes downstairs into Rekha's garden.

The unseasonable storm has only just begun, but already several saplings look mauled. The green-brown summer lawn is a whispering, shifting sheet of dry leaves.

Secrets. Whispers. Then the terror of a permanent silence.

There is another storm he remembers, an unseasonable storm embedded in his memory, a signpost tailor-made for crossroads. The storm broke the day his father did not return from his journey.

Shiv has spent a lifetime trying to reconstruct what his father did, what he said, what he was. But he has lost the day he lost him. All reconstruction ends at the point when the sky abruptly grows dark in the late afternoon.

It is this storm Shiv remembers vividly, not the words his uncle used to break the news, or his mother's wails, or his own reaction. His childish grief. What he remembers instead is what he sees again now.

Trees sway. The wind rustles wordless, horrific secrets. Once again he hears rain before he can see it. Droves of dragonflies trace the same agitated circle. The light is strange, silvery. It is a light in which dreams grow, thrive, and turn into nightmares.

Shiv freezes; his muscles grow taut in anticipation. Then Meena calls him from her room, as if she has sensed the nightmare memory plans to unravel for his benefit. He turns and sees her balanced on her crutch, standing at the window of her room.

The curtain is open, and so are the glass panes of the window. But the mosquito screen comes between her and the stirring world outside. It reminds Shiv of old black-and-white films in which gorgeously dressed upper-class women sit bored to death in their palatial rooms. Their only entertainment is looking at the world outside, the real world where men live and act, through the patterns of peepholes cut into the wall.

Shiv goes to Meena and helps her down the single step into the garden, not an easy thing because she is heavy. He staggers as she leans against him. "No one can accuse me of being a lightweight," she says with a grin, then falls silent as she takes in the splendor of the garden in disarray.

They hear a drawn-out groan and a rattle, as if a decrepit man is dying. Then a series of creaks, the last words of a sturdy house cracking at its foundations. But it is only a skinny papaya tree, its trunk snapping neatly at its waist. The tree trunk splits, the top half falls lightly to the ground like a dispensable twig. The very next moment they hear a wheeze of relief.

The fragrant hedge of Night Queen bends low, sweeping the ground.

The peacocks set up a screech. Their wail begins on a grief-stricken note as they scurry for safety, half-running, half-flying, their long tails tripping them up. But once they are safe, clinging clownishly to their swaying branches, their cry changes pitch. It is now a gloating, triumphant chorus of exultation.

Meena turns to Shiv, raises her hand to the empty skin where his mustache used to be. Then her hand moves up to his head, picks out the dry leaves from his hair with a gentleness he had not thought her capable of. He quells a passing moment of self-consciousness about his thinning hair; she has already seen more of him than incipient paunch and baldness.

Babyface joins them. He too has been drawn by nature's dramatic boogie-woogie in the backyard. He has deserted his wildly flapping tent in the front of the house, his chronic boredom forgotten. He has the same boyish, hopeful look on his face that he usually saves for his favorite TV show.

Together they watch the storm, Meena, Shiv and Babyface. Meena leans against Shiv, her upturned face filled with frank, sensuous enjoyment of the sound and fury about them. Storms, or Shiv's memory of them, will never be the same again. This is what it must be like to perform a funeral rite for a father.

As the cry of the peacocks fades, as the wind dies down, Shiv feels he is saying goodbye to his father for all time. He is finally ready to let go of his patchy memories of him—memories made up of frayed bits and pieces, blank spaces, stitches coming loose, knots unraveling. Just when Shiv is on the verge of living up to his father's ideals—though in a mock-heroic way—his father leaves with the storm; this time, it would seem, forever.

A few months after his father disappeared, Shiv tried, just once, to communicate with him.

Shiv's mother was sure her husband was alive, that she would hear from him in a day or two, a month, a year. She didn't just believe this; she made sure she put her act of faith on record. She sustained her belief for three years, spending most of her waking hours praying in the puja room. Then she slipped away without anyone in the house noticing, as if ashamed she could not stay on to prod her husband to come back, or plead with the gods to let him return. Shiv found her dead in the puja room, sitting rigid on the floor, eyes closed. She gripped the big brass puja bell so firmly that he had to pry it out of her lifeless hand.

Shiv's uncle, never one for exercises of the imagination, disapproved of this show of determined hope. As far as he was concerned, Shiv's father was declared dead a month after his disappearance. The uncle became Shiv's surrogate father; Shiv resented him, but secretly he took the uncle's part against his mother. Shiv believed his uncle the instant he said Shiv's father was dead. Shiv wanted his mother to give up the hope that festered like an open wound in their midst. But he also wanted her to have something else, something in place of what would be taken from her.

The uncle's daughter Rohini, two years older than Shiv, boasted that she had made a planchette board; she claimed she knew how to talk to the dead. One night, they sat in a circle in a locked room, the cousin, her sister, Shiv and two of his friends. The lights were switched off. The lone candle cast the appropriate flickering light on the board with its letters of the English alphabet and a rupee coin to be used as a counter. Shiv's right hand was on the board; the others placed their right hands on his, inches away from the coin.

"Uncle," the cousin whispered to the coin. "Do you have something to tell your son Shiva?"

They waited. The candle spluttered; they heard nothing else, except for their collective breathing.

Shiv couldn't bear to have his father fail him again. Shiv moved his hand slowly toward the coin, the weight of the other hands on top of his. He touched the hard edge of the coin and pushed it gently toward the letter Y. Just as they got to the letter E, the silence broke; the room resounded with an exultant bray, loud and endless.

They had forgotten to shut the window; they had also forgotten the donkeys that grazed in the maidan nearby. The cousin looked up from the board; her eyes met Shiv's. Then her mouth twitched and she burst into uncontrollable giggles. Soon they were all shaking with laughter as if they had never heard a donkey bray before.

Shiv never found that message in time, the right words he could carry to his mother, to fill her hands with something more than empty hope. He never found a way to lure his father back in solid flesh, or in audible words that would banish his own grief forever. But all these years later, he knows that when he remembers his father, he is speaking for his father as well as for himself. The father's voice, the voice of the remembered, is a part of his own voice. This is his father's legacy to Shiv: the gift of remembrance. He is in the past; in a closed room, the door never to be opened again. But Shiv can see him; he can know him, and anyone from the past he remembers, as part of himself. Whether Shiv is adulatory or critical, the remembered and the rememberer are bound together.

Shiv decides to postpone his visit to the Department. Instead he goes for a long walk alone. The air is fresh, as if the summer has finally admitted to being used up and made way for early winter. It is time to take stock: Shiv is now a living, contesting historian. Kin to the heroes of our times, a newcomer in that family peopled by reluctant, accidental members. His father, wherever he is, would have approved. But he is gone. Meena too will go, go back to her life, leaving him to hold on to his raggedy bit of heroism as best he can. And Rekha—she will be back soon to be treated to a close-up view of a husband who has momentarily shed predictability. Will she surprise Shiv as much as he will surprise her? Or will she want to pick up the pieces and restore order instantly?

But something will remain; something new must remain entirely his own. There is a time—the space of a day, a year, a moment—waiting with the patience of fate in every human life. A moment of discovery, irreversible, so that when you try to return to the business of ordinary living, you find your old life has been misplaced.

Even Shiv, despite a long record of lost opportunities, has found his way to the brink; from where he can, if he dares, make the necessary leap off the precipice. He has used his father's memory like a walking stick en route to this first-time risk-taking venture. It is Meena who put this stick in his hand again, coaxed his limping legs in the direction he knew—better than she—must be taken. Now the stick is superfluous. This is what Meena and her unlikely allies in contingency, his father, Basava, and the thought-policing touts of the Itihas Suraksha Manch have forced Shiv to see. Once he throws away all safe crutches, he can truly walk in the present. Be free to be curious, to speculate; to debate, dissent. Reaffirm the value of the only heirloom he needs from the past, the right to know a thing in all the ways possible.

TWELVE

OCTOBER 14–22

*O*nce more Meena is getting into the Maruti with her encased leg. It is amazing how easy it is this time. Meena does not groan or grimace or use the foul language Shiv hates associating with those ripe fruity lips. It helps that he can hold her as she crawls in, without having to be careful to avoid skin-to-skin contact. They have finally learnt how to make the entire operation simpler.

In the hospital too, everything goes smoothly. They are told they need not wait for the busy doctor. A junior doctor and a nurse will take care of removing the cast.

Meena is delighted. "Perfect!" she says to Shiv, "I don't want that creep ruining such a happy morning."

Still, when the young doctor arrives with what looks like an electric drill, Shiv longs to go looking for the seniormost fellow in the place, someone who inspires more confidence than this puppy whose medical degree is probably ten days old. But he forces himself to keep still. He contents himself with standing close to the table Meena lies on. She looks at Shiv, takes in his palpable anxiety, and grins teasingly. But when he takes her hand, she lets it rest in his.

Meena pulls up her skirt.

The drill splutters its way down her thigh, then her foreleg. The plaster gives way; the nurse removes the cast and drops it on the floor.

Meena props herself on her elbows and looks down at her leg. "Awful, isn't it," she says dispassionately.

Shiv says nothing, though he sees what she means. Alongside the healthy leg, this one looks terrible. The skin is shriveled, gray-white and flaky with dead skin, bits of thread and cotton fluff. Shiv only realizes the other leg is not naturally smooth when he notices the stubble of hair struggling out of the newly exposed, scaly skin.

The nurse catches him looking and frowns.

His eyes obediently move from Meena's leg to the floor where the cast lies. In spite of weeks of intimacy, the cast has already lost the shape of Meena's leg. The wild-colored garden Meena, Babli and Shiv planted on its dry surface has been uprooted. Some of the colors have faded. Others have run into each other from exposure to water. The imaginary garden that drew them together that dreamlike morning lies used up on the floor, as dispensable as the removed cast. The images they filled in with color have been ripped apart. The ground the painted flowers and leaves grew out of has split open.

Shiv moves to the stiff, hollow tube and picks it up, suddenly intolerant of such untidiness. He has never seen a silkworm's empty cocoon, but that is what the torn shell in his hand brings to mind. Later, as he goes to fetch the car for

Meena, he finds he is still holding the cast. Cast off, he thinks; cast away; castaway. He considers all three forms of the word with loathing; then he puts the broken thing away in the boot of his Maruti and locks it in.

The cast has come off. Meena is getting to know her leg again. She lavishes care on its dry, hungry skin. Kamla and she are closeted together in the bathroom for long sessions with oil, lotion, sponge and loofah. The leg no longer looks like the other leg's impoverished twin. The scales have fallen. The skin is now as smooth and silky as that on the healthy leg.

But Meena is also a stern taskmaster. She showers attention on the prodigal leg, but she expects it to reciprocate. Move as she wills it to. But to her indignation, the leg is both painful and disobedient. "It won't listen to me," she mutters like a bewildered, disappointed parent. She bites her lip as she tries forcing the leg to obey her commands.

"I knew that doctor was a bastard," she says bitterly. "He didn't say a thing about how difficult it would be to walk again."

But Shiv can see that despite all her complaints about how slow and painful it is, she will soon be on her feet again. Like the cast, the crutch will soon be cast aside. Already she shoos him away if he tries to help her.

"Let me do it alone," she hisses though he can see from her set face that she needs help. His days as Meena's guardian are numbered. Soon she will walk again, walk on. Walk away.

And Shiv? The storm helped him postpone his visit to the university to meet the Head. He has made a request for another appointment, this time with the entire trinity, the VC, the Dean and the Head. But he has not yet followed it up. Meena's exercises to reactivate her leg, her desire to discard the hated single crutch, her impatience to be done with it all, to get on with her life, to get back to it—his days are filled to the brim with Meena's preoccupations. With her determination to push convalescence into fast-forward mode. Her single-minded wooing of strength and well-being. And most of all, her energetic, obsessive pursuit of independence.

A week has passed, and it's Sunday again. A holiday. Perhaps he will look back on his time with Meena, sitting idle in his waiting room in purgatory, as a month of Sundays. Kamla too is on holiday. Without a qualm, as if he has been doing it all his life, Shiv cooks a large breakfast for Meena. In the midst of the food laid out on the table—an omelet, slices of hot buttered toast, orange juice, hot chocolate—he places a solitary sunny-yellow flower, a victim of the recent storm, in a little vase. The apples he has sliced lie on the plate in a red-skinned, fanlike cascade.

Meena walks slowly—minus crutch—to the table where Shiv waits for her. She sits down and eyes the laden table with approval. He exhales; he had not realized he was holding his breath.

As always, she eats with concentration, as if she must possess all tastes and flavors instantly and entirely. Shiv watches her silent, absorbed chewing, an image he has come to know so well.

Once she has drunk every drop of the frothy hot chocolate, she puts down the mug and turns to him. "Shiv, I spoke to Amar on the phone last night. He's got a friend's car for the day. He's going to take me back to the hostel this morning."

Shiv sits silent, watching her gladness. Her leg has been liberated from the oppressive cast. Though still painful, it is getting better every day. Meena's eyes are bright; she doesn't need him any more. His own little trouble has not been resolved, but he has taken a stand of resistance; Meena can now make believe he doesn't need her any more either.

The chocolate has left bubbly whiskers on her upper lip. He longs to wipe them away.

He looks at her as if his hand has moved, as if all it has to do is reach out to touch her. As if it has begun at her upper lip and traced a line down the stubborn chin and the fine edge of her jaw. The hand slides the curve of her proud neck, her strong shoulders, then lingers at the heavy breasts topped with rich brown nipples, the gently swelling smoothness of the belly with the perfect swirl of a button at its center. His hand moves down, travels around those wide hips, between the dangerous, generous legs, before it slips down her ankles to her earthbound feet.

His hand crawls off her toes and lands on the floor, letting her go. His hungry hand evaporates. He looks up from the floor and meets her eyes.

What can he say? And what difference does it make whether she leaves today, tomorrow or next week? She has to go back; he has to go on. Already he is learning to miss her.

Then he thinks of Amar spiriting her away. Confident Amar, who knows what it is to act, whether it is in love or on the streets. Ruthless Amar, so-very-young Amar. It's not a simple jealousy Shiv feels for Amar, not the age-worn, sexual jealousy of one man for another, or shop-soiled age for youth. What Shiv finds puzzling is that he is almost as fascinated by Amar as he is by Meena.

Shiv waits in the garden—what remains of it—while Meena packs. The sun is still high up in the sky, directly overhead, though it is an hour or more past noon. Though it is the third week of October, it is again so humid that the moist ground is fairly steaming. Clumps of striped brown worms writhe in the grass. The whole world, after its brief intermission of cool wind and shower, is on the boil again, seething with life.

He can hear the doorbell. Just a few hours ago he would have dashed to the door to save Meena a painful trip from her room. But now he finds it impossible to move—or move in time. Turning back, going into the house, facing Amar, facing Meena's goodbye. The images of the imminent future, the next fifteen minutes, flash past at lightning speed. It is the present that is played out in slow motion. It is this endless moment Shiv must step out of, this great bubble holding him in its sticky embrace, preventing him from going to her.

Look, the world, in a swell of waves, is beating upon my face. For a minute Shiv in his bubble sees Basava's end with startling clarity, a sharpness he has not been able to bring to his tentative narratives of his father's last day. Shiv sees Basava, an exhausted, frail reed by the river, a reed that still breathes. But the reed bends—how low it bends, letting the night air whistle through its skin, letting the whispering river flow over its feet. Basava takes a step forward, the river cool around his ankles, then flowing coolly round his knees. The river's wet fingers flutter round his thighs. *Today my body is in eclipse. When is the release, O lord of the meeting rivers?* Basava adds step by step; the river murmurs its approval; it surges forward. The river takes Basava in its arms, hushes all his last-minute plaintive cries. It is time to come together at last, to embrace that long-promised reprieve from interminable questions. The river, the river's watery void, glows. Then the world, the known world, pales.

. . .

But in another city, another millennium, everything around Shiv remains persistently alive and separate. Rekha's garden, the campus, the world beyond with its untasted delights and dangers, remain perversely colorful. Everything this sunny afternoon is flux, motion. The birds' full-throated chatter, the leaves' rustling, the awkward jerky movement of grass blades weighed down by scurrying ants and worms turning earth—all urge Shiv forward. *(The root is the mouth of the tree: pour water there at the bottom and, look, it sprouts green at the top.)* He too must become a part of this gigantic movement-loving ball rolling ahead purposefully. Like all living creatures going about their business as if fate does not lie waiting for them, he too must move, consign the puny self, its weak-hearted hesitations, to oblivion.

Shiv takes a step forward, stiff with self-consciousness. He bends his head, as if he has to walk uphill against a pushing, bullying wind.

The door to Meena's room is shut. He can hear animated voices, Amar's and hers. A theatrical exaggerated groan from her, then laughter.

Shiv takes a deep breath, straightens his back. When he knocks, their voices fall silent.

In the room, Meena's room, their room, Amar and Meena sit on the bed, waiting for Shiv.

Amar gets up when Shiv enters the room and greets him courteously. He calls Shiv *sir.* He is smooth, this champion of Meena's who has both words and passion at his fingertips. Politically committed *and* a gentleman if occasion calls for one. A well-brought-up hero.

Shiv returns his greeting but his eyes do not meet Amar's. Or Meena's. Instead they dart about the room. It is a strange, empty hole. No longer his study, no longer Meena's room. No longer his refuge, his sanctuary from the predatory world outside its walls. The room, the house, was so full of her things, of her, for the past few weeks. But he sees now, with astonishment, with a sickening lurch in his stomach, that everything that belongs to her has fitted into a suitcase and two open-mouthed plastic bags.

"Shall we go?" Amar, having made a few polite gestures in Shiv's direction, is finished with him.

Amar gets up, puts out a hand to help Meena. "Where's your crutch?" he asks her. "You had better take it with you." Shiv hears the undercurrent of authority in Amar's voice and winces, though he hardly knows why.

"I don't want it," Meena snaps at Amar. "I hate it. And why are you in such a hurry?"

Amar sits down abruptly and begins drumming on the table with long, nervous fingers. There is an awkward silence, the kind of pause when each one is waiting for the other to go first. To make a fool of himself first.

The awkwardness has touched Amar too. Suddenly he no longer looks so sure of himself. Shiv finds himself warming to him; Amar is only a boy. A precocious, dazzling fellow who may yet grow into a powerful man. But for now he is still a boy, learning his way through the labyrinth all men must travel.

Amar looks at Meena now—as if Shiv is not in the room—with a visible mixture of aggression and pleading. "Manzar is in the car," he says. "I asked him to wait there. I told you he has to return the car to his brother in a couple of hours."

"All right," agrees Meena, though there is nothing in common between her words and the challenging look in her eyes.

"You take my bags to the car and wait for me. I'll be there in a minute. I'll—Shiv will help me to the car."

Amar's eyebrows rise a fraction. He is on the verge of a retort, but swallows the argument ready on his lips. He shrugs, gets up. He takes the suitcase in one hand, the two plastic bags in the other. He leaves the room without a word to Shiv.

Meena and Shiv consider each other, wary, unsmiling.

Then she gets off the bed with a barely suppressed groan and stands. "Maybe I do need the crutch," she says.

Her voice is low and husky as if she has just woken up. All the certainty that is second nature to her, all the challenge that she exhales with every breath, has deserted her for the moment.

"Wait," Shiv says, and reaches for his father's walking stick propped up in a corner of the room. It has been there all the days and nights Meena was in his house, watching over her. Watching out for both of them.

"It's your father's, isn't it?" she asks him. Her hand curls around the hooked knob and covers it. "I'll take good care of it."

"I know you will," he says. He is not sure why they are both whispering.

She leans on the stick and hobbles closer to him. She stops. Their faces are just a few inches apart.

She steps back, places a gentle hand on his cheek in a brief, almost maternal caress. "Don't come with me," she whispers. "I can manage."

He nods.

She limps past him, out of the room.

He can hear his father's cane, now Meena's, tap its way out of the house. Then he hears the door shut behind her.

Acknowledgments

The lines by Zbigniew Herbert are from his poem "Report from the Besieged City" (*Report from the Besieged City and Other Poems,* translated by John Carpenter and Bogdana Carpenter, The Ecco Press, New York, 1958, p. 77) and are reprinted with the permission of the publishers. The lines by Busava ("The mind is the snake; the body is the basket . . .") are from vachana 160, translated by Kamil V. Zvelebil (*The Lord of the Meeting Rivers: Devotional Poems of Basavanna,* Motilal Banarsidass/UNESCO, Delhi, 1984, p. 31), and are quoted with permission from the publishers. All the other vachanas by Basava quoted in this novel are from A. K. Ramanujan's translations in *Speaking of Siva,* Penguin Books Ltd., Harmondsworth, 1973, pp. 67–90, and grateful acknowledgment is made to the publishers for their permission to use these extracts. In 1974, when I was a student in Bombay, a friend gave me a copy of Ramanujan's book, and this inspiring translation of medieval vachanas was my introduction to the poetry and ideas of Basava. Now, more than twenty-five years later, I find that my pleasure in these translations, and my gratitude for them, endures.

My understanding of Basava's ideas and poetry, his life and times, owes a great deal to other books too, including R. Blake Michael's *The Origins of Virashaiva Sects* (1992), J. P. Shouten's *Revolution of the Mystics* (1995) and Kamil V. Zvelebil's *The Lord of the Meeting Rivers* (1984). I am also grateful to the Kannada poet and playwright H. S. Shivaprakash, who shared with me his impressive knowledge of vachanas and virashaivism, as well as his own encounter with censorship some years ago.

But *In Times of Siege* is a work of fiction. It has used a variety of sources to imagine a life of Basava in a way meaningful to our times. Any resemblance to real individuals, places and events is purely coincidental. The same, alas, cannot be said for any resemblance to real-life ignorance, prejudice or bigotry.

ABOUT THE AUTHOR

Githa Hariharan was educated in Bombay, Manila, and the United States. She has worked in public television in the United States and as an editor in India. Her first novel, *The Thousand Faces of Night,* won the Commonwealth Writers Prize. Since then, she has published a collection of short stories, *The Art of Dying,* and two novels, *The Ghosts of Vasu Master* and *When Dreams Travel.* She lives in New Delhi.

A NOTE ON THE TYPE

This book was set in Adobe Garamond. Designed for the Adobe Corporation by Robert Slimbach, the fonts are based on types first cut by Claude Garamond (c. 1480–1561). Garamond was a pupil of Geoffrey Tory and is believed to have followed the Venetian models, although he introduced a number of important differences, and it is to him that we owe the letter we now know as "old style." He gave to his letters a certain elegance and feeling of movement that won their creator an immediate reputation and the patronage of Francis I of France.